Side by Side

ISABEL MILLER

Side by Side

Published in Great Britain by The Women's Press Ltd, 1996
A member of the Namara Group
34 Great Sutton Street, London EC1V 0DX

First published in the United States of America by The Naiad Press,
Inc, 1986

First published in Great Britain by Black Swan, 1991

British Library Cataloguing-in-Publication Data
A catalogue record for this book is available from the British Library

ISBN 0 7043 4446 7

Printed and bound in Great Britain by BPC Paperbacks Ltd

The quote on page 72 is from a sonnet by William Wordsworth, "Earth has not anything to show more fair."

The quote on page 212 is from G. I. Gurdjieff.

*To Miss Willson and Miss Brundige,
in the hope that
you will accept this as the book
you asked me for;
to Julie, for making me calm enough
to write;
to Elisabeth, for not letting me be
too calm;
to Natalie, Joyce, Charlotte, Louise,
Glenna, and Meg, because you didn't
give up on my education;
to Billie, for being bountiful with
your hard-won lore.*

Side by Side

BOOK ONE

BOOK ONE

CHAPTER ONE:
Sharon

I can't remember a time when I didn't know
Patricia Burley. I'd go further and claim there was
never a time when I didn't, but Patricia doesn't like
me to be a nut, so I go along with her all the ways I
can. There's enough ways I can't without adding any
on purpose. So I hardly ever mention — no more
than a couple times a year — that I'm sure we've
been born and born and born for each other and
she's tried to boss me every time. She always has to

3

be older, to have the upper hand. "You couldn't wait six lousy months!" I say, and she gets a look like I've really gone round the bend but she'll let it pass one more time.

I want us to be born at the same moment and have our mothers share a hospital room and fall in love with each other. That's my idea of a good start in life, and one of these times we'll get it right.

But this time is good. I'm not complaining. We even grew up across the street from each other, and as soon as I could walk I was trying to get to her. I already knew she was mine. She knew it too, but being older she made me be the one that did the courting. Mama said she was always having to grab me by the diaper to keep me out of the street.

"Why didn't you just take me across? I would've stayed," I said.

Mama said, "Patricia's folks didn't like us. They didn't like the truck."

Pa's oil truck, that is. The Burleys bought their house in the daytime while the truck was out on its rounds with Pa. Here was this quiet, leafy, red-brick street full of big solid old houses, just the place for a university family, they must have thought. How could they guess that an oil-delivering family would live there too and park its stinking truck at the curb every night at six? I think they blamed democracy, not knowing the whole cause was Patricia and me working our way closer to each other.

I was just as stubborn as Mama was shy, and she finally had to get up her nerve and ask Patricia's mother if she could put me in the back yard with Patricia. I want to cry when I think of Mama afraid of Mrs. Burley, putting on a clean dress, putting a clean sunsuit on me, so we wouldn't seem oily.

Mrs. Burley wasn't all that bad. Who wouldn't hate living with an oil truck? We didn't like it either, as a matter of fact.

Mrs. Burley was never super clean, specially when she was working on her house, bringing it back up to where it started. She was a little too shortish and roundish to climb ladders, but she did, a lot, and got dusty and sweaty and so tired from peeling off old wallpaper that she didn't wash dishes. But she did have a fancy air about her even so — she was a doctor of philosophy, like Mr. Burley, but the university had a rule against hiring a husband and wife both, so the only use she could make of her academic gown was to dress up as a witch on Halloween.

Mama didn't know from Ph.D.'s, but she knew there was something scary about Mrs. Burley. So Mama stood there choked up, waiting for an answer, and I stood there hugging her leg. Even in diapers, I was ready to kill anybody that hurt my mother.

Patricia was a shortish squarish baby giving me a look with one shiny-bright brown eye between the pickets of the backyard fence. I don't really remember it, but I can see that eye anyhow, and that half-grown-in red hair, still downy.

She claims to remember. She claims she was thinking, "What took you so long? Where have you been?"

"Well," Mrs. Burley said, too slow, probably reminding herself of democracy and that Patricia had all her shots. "Well, of course," she said. "That would be nice." Mama lifted me over the fence and Patricia and I began another lifetime of being side by side.

With gaps. Like exchange professorships, when her family would go to a foreign country for a whole year. I hate that about university people. Like summer. The Burleys had a place on a lake out in Michigan where they went as soon as school was out. Mr. Burley had summers off, except some wonderful years when he taught summer school. He was hairless and shortish and squarish. My Pa never said "the Burleys." He always said "the Dumpies." How tall you were was pa's main way of telling if you were any good.

Us tall Almos never went anywhere, even though the oil business slacked off in summer and we could have. During the war, Pa had seen the world and he didn't like it. He liked his life just like it was, don't move a thing. Sometimes he did take us for a Sunday drive, because Mama liked to look at other people's houses, but he kept the ballgame on the car radio the whole time so it was no fun and it sure didn't count as a trip.

I thought I just pined for a trip. I wanted to be un-hicky, like Patricia. I wanted her to be home sometimes and me not, so she'd know how it felt. But I have to admit it, I ended up quite a lot like Pa. If I can be in my home with my mate, I want nothing but to stay right where I am.

Patricia used to read to me. Reading aloud was what her family did for entertainment, like my family watched television. They were copying some bygone time they liked better. Their furniture was old-timey, too, and Mrs. Burley washed and ironed cloth handkerchiefs because Kleenex, to them, was in a class with TV.

Even as a baby, Patricia was careful with books. She'd wash her hands and make me wash mine before we touched a book, and then we'd sit together on that hard slippery black couch and hold the book across our legs and she'd jabber away. She couldn't read. Hell, she couldn't talk. But she threw in question marks and exclamations and sometimes she'd stop importantly and point to a picture, which would be black and white and brainy, because these were books her parents had as children, maybe her grandparents too, for all I know, and not bright and funny like the Little Golden Books Mama bought for me at the grocery. Patricia had to stop whining for Little Golden Books, because her father said she couldn't play with me anymore if she didn't cut that out.

Later we painted too. Mr. Burley didn't believe in coloring books. Patricia was crazy about mine, and my crayons. She thought they were naughty and therefore sexy. She agreed with her father that a child should have plain white paper of good quality and watercolors and a little smock that closed in the back with one button. We did some nice pictures. Her father saved them all, even mine, and wrote our ages on them. There's one I did when I was three that's the most joyful thing I ever saw. It's a round smiling face with legs — no body, just this big circle done in one sweep and a mess of jumbled hair, and legs bent to feet at the ends. Patricia tells me that the Chinese symbol for the Heavenly Way is a head with legs, and I think that painting shows I had some wisdom in me then. More than I have now.

Patricia painted princesses, one after another. Armies of princesses, all red-haired like her and in jewelled gowns. She's embarrassed now at that one-track mind, but I think she knew something then, too.

The TV said the Queen of England was paying us a visit. Us personally, we thought, and got so excited we couldn't sleep. Take Christmas and double it. Now again. That's how excited we got. We looked forward to meeting our own kind. Patricia tried to teach me to curtsey, but why should I curtsey when she wasn't planning to? If she could look the Queen in the eye and talk shop, so could I. She said the Queen might not recognize us right away and we wouldn't want to make her mad by me not curtseying.

Then the TV was making a fuss over a dowdy little woman in a plain hat and a housedress. No crown, no robe, no jewels, no long train held up by cute little princesses, and she had come to see President Eisenhower, not us. *"That's* not the Queen," Patricia said. I knew it was the Queen and that Queens were a gyp and I gave up on them, but Patricia said no, there was just some mistake, and we went over to her house so she could paint a real Queen and put this phony out of her mind.

Later Patricia moved on to ballerinas, to paint and to be. I'd sit on the floor beating time with my hands and singing, and she'd lunge around. I was actually a better dancer, and still not very good, but I almost always had to be the orchestra, so she could show her mother she was really talented and should have ballet lessons, it would be a crime to neglect such a talent.

Before long Mrs. Burley gave in, and Mama did, and we were spending our Saturday mornings in the upstairs of a store downtown, placing our feet this way and that and holding our arms up. It was all kind of a letdown, not a bit like flying, but we hung in because we'd whined so much to get there. If our folks found out we hated it, they might have an excuse not to give us the next thing we whined for. But one Saturday morning when the teacher walked along the line of girls, correcting our positions, she gave Patricia's leg a tap with her stick, and that did it. Nobody hits Patricia.

I was just as glad. All the good TV shows were on Saturday morning. Mrs. Burley was glad too, I think. She always wore her raincoat when she drove us to dancing class, even on the hottest days, to hide her grungy clothes. And Mama was glad, because it wasn't easy to get the money for my lessons out of Pa.

He didn't even want to send me to kindergarten, which you had to pay for while us Baby Boomers were overloading the schools. My teacher friends tell me that even now when a school board has to economize, the first thing it thinks of is dropping free public kindergarten.

"Private kindygarden? Money for kindygarden? What is this shit?" Pa yelled. He had the money, but he's a man of principle. He said he would keep his money and teach me himself.

"I'll be glad to lay a little mat on the floor so Sharon can take a little nap, and when she wakes up I'll be glad to give her a tambourine to pound on and we'll march around."

What he meant was Mama should, somebody whose time wasn't valuable.

He gave Mama quite a fight, but the September I was five and Patricia was almost six, we started private kindergarten together. Her six-month head start hadn't done her a bit of good when it came to school. Next time she'll know not to be born in February.

I never understood, even after she told me, what she had against her mother. I was so crazy about mine, so quick to be mad if I thought somebody was putting her down, so comforted against her body, so afraid she'd die having all those babies, so much on her side when she fought with Pa, so aching for her to have the things she liked or wanted, such as underpants with flowers embroidered on them, even if they were silly and cost more. Patricia was my first lesson, but not my last of course, in how it takes all kinds.

She actually plotted against her mother, and passed her plots on to me because she took it for granted I'd want to do the same to mine. Always have to peepee when you go downtown or to a movie or restaurant, she told me, and always save a little so you can do it again real soon. Never pass a drinking fountain without making her hold you up to it. Every little drop helps with the peepee, and even if you're not thirsty and can't drink any, she won't know the difference and you can always get water all over your face and clothes. Sneak off to school early so you can wear your big brother's argyle socks (I had no brother, so Patricia advised me to wear my father's) and everybody will think you're a poor neglected child. Put your shoes on the wrong feet, ditto. Ask the neighbors for food. When you bring the mail in, take the magazines to your room and have a fit about your privacy if she brings them out. Tell her you took poison.

That one didn't work. Most of Patricia's plots were the kind that even when her mother saw through them she couldn't do anything. Like if she said no, I just took you to the bathroom, Patricia could wet her pants and be in the right. But when Patricia came in sobbing and gagging, trying to puke, saying she'd eaten a tulip bulb (because the TV said they were poison), Mrs. Burley didn't even get down off her stepladder. "Show me," she said. "Bring it to me," and we went back outside and searched around and finally Patricia decided on a promising-looking leaf and slobbered on it and took it to her mother. "It's a daylily," her mother said and kept on painting the wall. "Isn't that lucky? You won't have to go to the hospital and have your stomach pumped. The Chinese eat them by the ton for breakfast."

Mrs. Burley didn't understand that Patricia wanted to have her stomach pumped, thought it would be fun. Usually Mrs. Burley understood Patricia inside out, and I think maybe that's the real reason Patricia gave her such a hard time. Patricia was just plain embarrassed at being crystal clear, no mystery.

"When Daddy comes home, he'll take me to the hospital!" she yelled, and we waited on the porch steps for Mr. Burley, who didn't understand anything about Patricia except that she was an absolute

darling, Daddy's beautiful treasure. Patricia was
drooling and trying to turn green, not knowing that
holding your breath turns you red.

"Why don't you like your mother?" I asked.

"She's stingy. She's dumb. She's not a real
Burley. She doesn't like Grandpa and Grandma
Burley. She doesn't like the Old Place."

"That's no reason," I said. I'd never seen the Old
Place, but I didn't like it either because it kept
Patricia away all summer. Would she not like me
either if she found that out?

"She's a sissy," Patricia said. "She just sits by
the lake with the mothers and babies and they just
talk about how they hate the Old Place. They're all
sissies. The worst thing is to belong with the sissies."

My mother was probably a sissy too, but she
didn't have to show it and I didn't care anyway. She
made up for it other ways.

Patricia said, "Mother always wants to stay here
and mess up the house and Daddy has to say, '*We
will go. We are going,*' and then she says bad things
about Grandpa and Grandma Burley because she's
dumb. She's not a true-born Burley. She's just a
Burley by marriage."

Then her cuckoo clock kooked four kooks and we
went over to my house to watch Popeye. She didn't
want to wait and tell her father she was poisoned
anyway. She didn't play tricks on him. He was a
king.

The trouble with watching Popeye was that my
little sisters were all over the place, and there were
always ads about how when The Bomb came you
should go to your basement or fallout shelter and you
should have food and water stored there so you

wouldn't die. The thought of having to go to the basement with my sisters just made me sick, and anyway we didn't have any food or water there. Patricia didn't have any in her basement either. We watched Popeye and worried and worried, and the funny part is, we didn't say a word about it to our folks. It was like a secret among children that The Bomb was coming.

Of course the teachers knew, because they had to show us how to crawl under our desks and hide our heads in our arms in case we were in school when The Bomb came. But parents didn't know, and we didn't want them to. I think we were afraid that if they knew and got worried, The Bomb would be really true. As long as they didn't know, there was still a chance The Bomb was a kind of Santa Claus, except bad — a story for children.

Some unlucky kids had houses on slabs, no basements, but they had to start lying and say they just got a basement, because everybody freaked at the sight of them, like they had a weird disease. Even while you were being really nice to them, you couldn't stop thinking how The Bomb was going to get them.

A movie at school showed soldiers washing the tires of cars that probably didn't even have any radioactive dust on them, just to be super careful. That was supposed to make us feel safe. The movie also showed a woman all housewifed-up in a headscarf and galoshes, admiring a box of really big red strawberries that had been treated with radioactivity so they would never rot. They were beautiful, like the ruby-red slippers of Oz, so appetizing, but, no matter what the movie said, by then we knew they were poison like Snow White's apple.

When older people say our generation had everything too easy and was plain spoiled, I always remember us crouched under our desks with our arms around our heads, and wonder what they think was so great about growing up when we did. I don't say it was worse to fear The Bomb than God and Hell like they did, or worse to have Vietnam than World War Two, but what makes them think we were too lucky for our own good? Can't they see there's always something? They regret they didn't put a few more hard knocks into our education. In fact, the best things we got we just took, in spite of them, such as gay rights. They'd like us better if we were struggling for food and shoes instead. They really hate it that we don't think an orange is a treat.

My house had TV, but Patricia's house was better because it had no pushy little sisters, just her shortish, squarish big brother Everett, who would not even look at us, and it had Patricia's own room with a door that shut. We played many games in it, not all sexy.

We played, for instance, Feet on the Wall. Laying — or as she taught me to say, *lying* — on her bed, one of us would make a dance pattern on the wall and the other had to copy it exactly. We played The President Is Coming to Dinner. In that one, we were Chef-Boy-R-Burley and Chef Boy-R-Almo and we used a dresser drawer as an oven and roasted a filthy old mildew-smelling earless and eyeless stuffed Easter

Rabbit and rushed around being afraid the President would arrive before it was ready. We also played Beauty Parlor, which sort of oozed over into sexy, at least for me. It just never got to Patricia like it did to me.

For me, the sound of a comb being dipped into water, clicking against the glass, is still enough by itself to set my scalp tingling. Then came the accidental icy drips on my neck and back, and Patricia braced against me giving me permanents, finger waves, comb waves, and spit curls, so clumsy and careful, trying so hard she forgot to swallow and had to slurp sometimes. Spit curls, especially in back where my hair meets my neck, were best.

Spit was good for Doctor, too. We never did what the real doctor did, which was weigh us and tell our mothers what fine specimens we were and bring us back in six months. ("Ask him if you can't just *mail* him the check," Pa said.) Our way of being a doctor was to split your belly open with a Popsicle stick, take out your appendix, and put you back together by sticking spitty toilet paper all over you. Or test your hearing by whispering in your ear. Or touch you all over with the tip of a watercolor brush and keep a record of where it felt best, such as ears, nipples, knee-backs, and pips. Patricia always called the pips "vulva" but I never would because it sounded cold. Rubbery. A terrible name for our cute neat warm pink cracks. They had so many good-feeling places inside that we had to keep track of them on a separate sheet of paper.

* * * * *

When I was about ten, Mama bought me a shirt
that had points all around the bottom like big saw
teeth, and even though it was ordinary cotton and
merely pale green, that bottom edge made it royal. It
became our King costume. Whoever wore it became
King Albert. The other by taking off all her clothes
became Queen JoAnn.

King Albert would throw open the door and stomp
in, very mad, complaining that the meals had been
terrible lately, the palace a mess, the handkerchiefs
not ironed, the crowns not polished, and he didn't
have a clean ermine robe. Was that any way to treat
somebody who had been writing laws all morning?
Queen JoAnn had better shape up.

She would be stretched out on the bed with her
arms behind her head so he could get a really good
view of her flat chest. She would blur her eyes and
look up at him and whine, "Albert, I'm cold. Don't
you have any heat in this palace?" King Albert would
fall on her with apologies and hugs, touching all the
places we'd learned about in Doctor, saying it was
okay about the food, it was okay about everything.
Then the Queen would get the shirt and become King
and we'd start over. It was our best game. It never
got boring. It lasted for hours. Nothing stopped us
except being called to meals. I don't think we ever
stopped of our own accord.

But for a long time we didn't kiss, except bare
skin. We didn't kiss lips or pips, because we were
scared of germs, especially Patricia. She'd been
warned about germs all her life and had even seen
them, in her brother Everett's microscope, blobbing
around with their little fangs and whiskers, and she
was really scared of them. I pretended I was too

because I didn't want her to think us Almos were slobs.

My family is as good as hers, but we don't let on.

Of course I knew perfectly well that germs can't hurt you unless you let them, and I especially knew Patricia's germs, in case she had any, would not hurt *me*. It was to show that an Almo could be as dumb about germs as a Burley that I let her wait so long to kiss my mouth.

We were about thirteen before she did, and still playing King Albert even though the King Albert costume had become dust rags long ago and would have been too small by then anyway. We didn't bother with the play-acting anymore either. We were down to the heart of the game, but still calling it King Albert — so we wouldn't have to call it making love.

One afternoon when she was lying on me and breathing into my ear, I felt a change in her body, like a decision, and she began to kiss my cheek, a whole row of flat little smacks heading in the general direction of my mouth, and then she backed off and asked, "Are you still scared of my germs?"

I said no. Right then I wasn't too interested in the Almo Family honor.

"I'm not scared of yours either," she said, and we both squeezed our eyes tight shut and our mouths tight shut. She gave me one shut-tight kiss and would have stopped there, but I had a good two-arm hug on her and held her down until we didn't feel silly and could open our eyes and mouths and be soft.

What a difference! There was her sparkly brown eye too close to focus, the red hairs of her eyebrow, the breath from her nose, the two wets of our mouths. We weren't turned on. It's like we were soul to soul and very quiet, except to say each other's names, Patricia and Sharon, not Albert and JoAnn.

I don't know what I mean by soul, but I don't know any other way to say it.

We had a little gang of girls our own age that did things like chop rivers in the ice so the streets could drain, and try to make dope out of chewing gum and bananas, and choose some teacher to get a mass groupie crush on.

Miss Roop, the gym teacher, was it that year. The rest of the gang would pair off any old way and pretend to be Miss Roop making out with a man, but Patricia and I paired off with nobody but each other.

Once when I was at bat and Becky was behind me being catcher, she said, "How come you and Patricia stick together so much?"

I said, "We do the same stuff, but we don't pretend we're somebody else," and let a very easy pitch go by.

"Gee, like my mother," Becky said.

We all knew the whole gang's family secrets. Her mother had left town with somebody else's mother. They were in New York being lesbians, which was an okay thing for them but seemed kind of eerie for Patricia and me, kind of too *old* for us, like foot trouble or something, like false teeth. Lesbians were older people, mothers. We were children playing.

"No, not like your mother," I said, taking a huge swing and missing.

"Ha ha! That's what you get for lying!"

So I told the truth. "*Sort of* like your mother," I said, but missed the next pitch anyway.

CHAPTER TWO:
Patricia

Daddy writes books that nobody buys. He has a
plan to induce the National Association of
Jerrybuilders to put at least ten feet of bookshelves
into every new house and then to carry out a massive
propaganda campaign in women's magazines saying
bookshelves must have books on them. Not dishes of
peanuts, *books*. Daddy's books are about Aaron Burr's
plot and Shays' Rebellion and the Battle of Fallen

Timbers, so they still might not get on many shelves, but they do get him promoted.

I always thought of Daddy's plan when I went to Sharon's house. It had built-in oak bookcases with glass doors, but on the shelves was Mrs. Almo's collection of salt and pepper shakers shaped like frogs and flowers and Mexican children of opposite sexes, the Leaning Tower of Pisa, the Statue of Liberty, snails, bears, and windmills, all spread out to try to fill the space. Those bookcases were big. The only printed words in the whole house were in the newspaper, *TV Guide,* and Little Golden Books.

To me it was an exotic world, like Samoa — all right, of course, just entirely different. Wall-to-wall beige carpeting (because beige goes with everything), beige chairs (to match the carpet) supersoft like clouds, beige draperies with pull cords, venetian blinds. I really liked Sharon's house. It had no paint cans, paint remover, bits of scraped-off wallpaper, dirty dishes, or unsorted junk mail. It had year-apart little girls giggling like Eskimos, rolling around and chewing on each other like a litter of puppies. It had an always-pregnant mother whose legs were wrapped in Ace bandages and whose face went sappy at the sight of Sharon, her tall, strong, petal-skinned, clean-moving masterpiece, her advocate, whose brown hair shed rainbows when the wind blew it across itself in sunlight.

I'd have been embarrassed to get such looks from my mother, but Sharon didn't even notice. In our family it was Everett who got those looks, and he didn't notice either. Once I overheard Mother telling a pregnant woman, wishing her a boy, "When the

doctor holds him up and you see that little penis, it's
your Ph.D. and your novel and your salon." When
Mother saw my little vulva, it was her unmade beds,
I bet, her whole despair of ever catching up. What
she has never understood is that we have everything
men have, but theirs has fallen out so it shows. She
needed a friend like Sharon to teach her how much
we have inside. She needed the Old Place, sooner,
before she was a mother, before it was too late.

The abstract of the Old Place's title starts with
the Indian cession to the French and then the French
grant to someone named Burley, and from then on
it's Burleys all the way. I love that place. Its purity.
Its sturdy ghosts. The land has grown back to pine,
which is all that wants to grow in that Michigan
sand anyway, and every summer the whole extended
Burley Family gathers there. The aunts and cousins
hang out in cabins or tents all summer, and the
uncles come on weekends, all who can. I always feel
sorry for those who through intermarriage to lesser
breeds have lost the name Burley. To this day I feel
I'm bragging when I say my name is Burley.

Part of the Old Place is a lake, also named
Burley. We're too modest to tell its name unless
someone is really wild to know and drags it out of
us.

I remember dozens of red-haired kids, big and
little together, my arrogant brother Everett, my
arrogant cousins, not making allowances for age or
sex, holding us to our history, our wonderful genetic
heritage. Anybody who couldn't keep up was dumped

contemptuously with the women. We ran in packs together in endless games, learned to be brave, to hold our breath under water for a long time, to sail, swim, row, whittle, sing harmony, play recorders and guitars, jump from high places, swing on a rope from one edge of the hayloft to the other or drop fearlessly into the dusty old hay, throw straight and far. We didn't tattle, didn't cry. We made the clean blue lake look rusty when all our red heads were bobbing in it.

I'm still trying to become worthy of my name and my red hair.

I've never asked anyone, except Sharon, to understand. We haven't produced anybody famous, or even rich. Our only difference is that we've stayed together and kept a record. We are simple and solid, good householders. Healthy. Competent. That's harder to live up to than you might think. It costs something. Sometimes it costs too much.

I did hope Sharon would understand that I couldn't, right away, bear to be somebody who couldn't go to the Old Place, but she preferred to be mystified, so she could keep on thinking our troubles were my fault.

Sharon created our troubles by loving and trusting her mother. The merest dog can recognize its natural enemy, but Sharon couldn't. I had tried for years to teach her, but she was beyond help in that respect. We had such a sweet thing going, and everybody was too busy to notice. We could have gone on forever. We weren't odd. We weren't obsessed. Inseparable, yes, but casual. We had our gang. We did the usual kid things. Boys came around. The sexual revolution was just starting. It wasn't mandatory yet. They didn't expect anything but food. They were okay. We liked some of them.

Sharon and I just lived, and holding one another was part of living. We were like horses standing together. Like monkeys searching one another's bodies for salt. Like hands. We just loved one another. We just ate one another's germs.

From the fuss, you'd have thought we were undermining Western Civilization. Who gets up these rules?

We had two good years.

Then it was the fall of the year we were fifteen. Maybe we had been a little too glad to see one another after my summer at the Old Place. Something had made Mrs. Almo, at last, wonder.

We came home from school and were leaping up the stairs to my room when Mother came out to the hallway. "Sharon," she said, as seriously as though there'd been a death, "your mother wants you to come right home."

"Sure," Sharon said, meaning pretty soon.

"Right away," Mother said.

Sharon went home and Mother gestured me to the living room, where Daddy and Everett were waiting for me. Why Everett? I guess when you undermine Western Civilization, it's everybody's business.

Daddy said, "Sharon's mother phoned today. Sharon has told her you two are doing some things you shouldn't."

My whole body went klunk, but I said nothing. I wasn't going to give them anything.

He said, "I'm not going to embarrass us all by

asking you about it. We've made an appointment for you to see a therapist. You can talk it all out with him."

"I won't go," I said.

"We can't force you to, of course, but I wish you would. Sharon will be seeing someone too. This is really very serious. I think you know it is. Why else would you have been so deceptive?"

"I won't go," I said.

Mother said, "Patricia, you're young. You're still malleable. You owe it to yourself to save yourself while you still can."

"I don't need saving," I said.

"Listen, young lady," Daddy said. "Don't kid yourself. This is a problem. It is a disease. It is a recognized disease with a name. Look it up. It is also, incidentally, a crime. So let's have no more bravado about not needing saving."

I gave him my most sullen look and said nothing.

He said, "You won't be able to get a good job. You may not even be able to get an education. People are expelled from school for this."

He had to be lying. The world couldn't be *that* crazy.

"And you won't be able to go to the Old Place, of course."

"What?"

"Nobody will want you around the children."

I was shocked and hurt enough to make him take some pity on me. "I don't mean to upset you. But I do think you'd better keep your appointment. We'll all back you up. We all want you to have a happy life. We all love you. Enough," he added with his little professor smile, "to have you tell a psychotherapist what a terrible family we are, if that will help you."

Everett looked the way he did when he and the cousins were dumping some sissy with the women and babies, entirely disgusted and contemptuous. "You make me sick," he said. That, at last, made me cry.

My parents could have sent me free to the university counseling service, so it was frightening that they paid actual money to a downtown shrink. Either they were ashamed to let anyone at the university know about me, or they thought my case was too desperate for a mere graduate student to practice on. More than anything they said, the money showed me how serious they were. The Burleys do not spend money lightly. They must really have thought I was in mortal danger. Even though I knew the idea was absurd, I had to be impressed. Getting them to stop watching me would not be easy.

The shrink was a young guy, quite cute in fact. He had a mustache, I suppose so he'd look a little older and more impressive, and maybe to show his male hormones were all there. It was red, though his head hair was brown. I figured he had some sympathetic genes somewhere.

His office still smelled of paint. I think he'd just moved in. I could have been his first client. I think my parents found him in the Yellow Pages. I know they didn't ask around among their friends.

"Well, let's begin," he said. "What brings you here?"

"Didn't they tell you?"

"Let's hear your side."

"Then they didn't tell you."

"Do you want them to have told me?"

"Sure. Then I won't have to."

"You're reluctant to speak of it?"

"Wouldn't you be?"

"Not to someone who could help me."

"The help I need is to get my parents off my back."

"Maybe we can do that."

I saw that he could, yes of course he could. I decided to be a good patient. If he wanted me to talk, I would talk, I would tell the truth. Lies were too complicated and would slow me down.

"Okay," I said. "I was doing stuff they didn't like. With my best friend. My ex-best friend. I used to love her, but now I'd like to smash her head. She ratted on us. She was stupid."

"Maybe that was her way of asking for help."

"Some help! It's her fault we're in this mess."

"Tell me about the mess."

Telling somebody did feel good. I babbled on and on. He got all excited about my hostility to my mother, my brother's being the favorite child and so on, but he sat almost still and just went "Umm?" to keep me babbling. The fifty minutes went fast. We ended up with him saying this particular mess needn't amount to much, but the life of a lesbian is one long mess.

That word was a shock. What did a word like that have to do with rolling around with Sharon a little?

He saw he'd shocked me, but he didn't back

down. He said, "Life's hard enough. Why be a lesbian if you don't have to?"

"That makes sense," I said. I'd seen too many shrinks drunk at my parents' parties to think they were all-wise and could read your mind.

"Give yourself a chance," he said. "Stay away from Sharon. Surround yourself with normal influences. Society will help you. Society is *designed* to help you. Wear some makeup. Wear skirts. Date some boys. Don't discuss your feelings with anybody but me. And I'll see you next week."

I nodded and started to leave, but he had one more thing to say. "Oh, Patricia, I almost forgot. We ask you not to read any psychological material right now. We need to insulate the therapeutic situation. I know you understand."

I understand now better than I did then. He didn't want me to read Carl Gustav Jung, who said he didn't know anything about the lesbian and neither did anybody else, but he suspected that her task was nothing less than to save humanity.

I was just barely home when the telephone rang. Mother and I both answered at the same time on separate extensions and heard the big he-man voice of Sharon's father saying, "Sharon's got something she wants to say. I'll be on the other phone."

He scared me so much that I was almost glad to have Mother with me on the line. I doubted I could say anything, but she could scare him right back, if necessary, with her Important Lady voice.

"Speak up, girl!" he said. "We're not going to make a habit of this."

Then Sharon was choking out, "I'm sorry! I'm sorry!" between sobs.

She was going at it all wrong. She was making our little games *important*, when everything depended on making them *un*important. She had absolutely no talent for guile.

I said, in a stiff phony voice, "It's okay. It's time to grow up now anyway."

"Please don't be mad at me," she sobbed.

"I'm not, but I want to grow up now."

"Promise you're not mad?"

Of course I was mad, but what difference did that make? It was not I who kept us apart.

I said, "I'm not, but I'm going to stay out of your way and I want you please to stay out of my way."

"You don't want to be my *friend?*"

"Maybe someday," I said.

She just sobbed. Her father said, "That's enough now."

I heard their two hanging-up clicks. Over the buzz of the dial tone, Mother said, "You're tough." How would a sweet gentle person have acted at a time like that, being sobbed at in front of hostile witnesses? Why should I have to feel guilty, when nothing was my fault?

Everything was Sharon's fault, for trusting her natural enemy, then for making a big tragic scene, but I was the one who felt guilty.

Sharon seemed dumb. I knew she really wasn't,

but right then she seemed dumb, and I can hardly
stand dumb people. For a while I didn't love her.

My fingernails grew long and I painted them. I
painted my lips and eyelids, too. My nice straight
heavy hair got cooked into curls and lost its
glossiness. It looked like an old woman's henna-dyed
hair. I wore narrow skirts that shortened and
tightened my steps and made my legs ache. I carried
a clutch bag.

So there I was, without the use of my hands or
legs and getting lipstick all over my food, and
everybody said how great I looked, what a welcome
change all this was. One by one my teachers took me
aside to compliment me, even Miss Roop. My parents
were relieved. My brother, probably coached to be
supportive, mumbled, "That's more like it."

I must have looked like the quickest cure in
history. I must have gone right to the shrink's head.
He must have felt like a damn sage. He probably
wrote a scholarly article about me.

Nobody seemed to notice I was depressed. Or else
nobody cared. I had to work to get my voice above a
whisper. I guess depression looks like femininity.

I used to lie in my friend Mike's arms and suck
his T-shirt. When we got up, his shirt would have big
wet rings around his nipples.

Mike was nice, but I couldn't really feel him or
love him. The world can embarrass you out of loving

somebody it doesn't want you to love, but it can't make you love the one it chooses for you. I doubt it cares much. What's love got to do with anything the world values?

The world can even make you believe that the right way to uphold your family's honor is to be a coward.

CHAPTER THREE:
Sharon

Mama cried a lot. I figured it was about me being a rotten person, and I just got madder at her. But when she calmed down enough to talk, she said, "I don't know how I came to do such a thing, Honey. I'm sorry, Honey," and I saw she was an ordinary hick dumbbell that had made an ordinary mistake out of plain dumbness. All my mad floated away. I hugged her and said, "It's okay, Mama," and I meant it. Not

that I didn't still have troubles, but it felt good not
to be mad at poor Mama.

One trouble was Pa. He took off his belt like he
was going to beat me with it. I was pretty sure he
wouldn't because he never had. He was a big yeller,
but he never hit us. He stood there whapping the
folded-up belt against his palm and saying a lot of
bad things that I didn't much listen to. I was too
busy keeping track of that belt. But I did hear a
little, like that a queer is worse than dirt and he'd
rather see me dead. Then he threaded the belt back
into his pants and said, "Your mother told them
damn Dumpies we'd send you to a crazy-doctor. Well,
there's never been a crazy Almo and we're not gonna
start now. You hear me?"

"Yes, Pa."

"I'm a respectable businessman. I've got my good
name to think of. When we have a problem inside of
our family we take care of it inside of our family. I
can straighten you out by myself, and you better
believe it. And when you come to your senses, you
can come into the business. You're the best I can do
with no boy. I want you to remember that. You can
be a pardner. But you got to straighten up."

"Yes, Pa."

"Now you get on up to your room and start
thinking about mending your ways."

I went to my room and plotted how to get
Patricia back. I knew crying wouldn't get anywhere
with her. I knew I had to make her laugh — had to
delight her. That was impossible right then when all
I had was tears.

My worst trouble was, she wouldn't speak to me.
I didn't see how she could help it, living right across

the street from me like that, but she managed. We'd
walk to school half a block apart and never speak.
Her new tight skirts made her walk so slow I had a
hard time staying behind her. I could go faster than
that hopping backwards on one foot. I'd slouch along
behind her and see her add on some new nonsense
every day — her hair even turned plain rusty and
stopped shining — and at night I'd sit in my room in
the dark and look at her window.

My sadness then was about like what a sad song
makes you feel. I mean, there was a corner of my
mind that liked it. I imagined some stranger might
look at me and ask, "Who is that beautiful girl and
what secret sorrow lurks in her tragic eyes?"

Then Mike started coming out of his house when
she passed and walking to school with her. He started
walking her home after school, too, and hanging out.
I stopped feeling like the star of a cute romance that
would all turn out right at the last minute. Seeing
Patricia and Mike came close to killing me. My chest
felt like some giant claw had grabbed my breastbone
and ripped it out and left me with a bloody hole
where it belonged. The pain was physical and terrible.
No part of me liked it. It was nothing to sing about.
I was afraid of it. I stopped looking at Patricia's
window. I walked to school along a different street.
Not seeing her helped some, but not enough. And I
was always scared I'd see her by accident and get
torn up. I really had to get away.

Pa wasn't letting me run with my gang anymore,
either. I needed to talk to Becky and tell her how
terrible I felt and cry and have her hold my head in
her lap and tell me I was a good person, but I

couldn't get away from Pa long enough, and I had to settle for writing Becky a note instead.

I pushed my note through the air vent of Becky's locker. Her answer was in my locker at the end of the next class. She said Patricia was really furious at me for blabbing to the wrong generation and messing us up. "Tough luck. I think it would help you to go see my mother," Becky wrote, and gave me her mother's address.

But how was I going to get down to New York? Pa wasn't letting me out of his sight except to go to school. I hate to admit how slow I was to see I could go to the Adirondack Trailways bus station instead of school. My brain is pitiful sometimes. I could be back home before Mama had much chance to worry, and what if Pa did beat me up? I could take it. Then the old slow brain chugged and gurgled some more and I saw I should find a job in New York, waiting tables or babysitting or like that, and just stay there, because New York was used to people like me. I'd heard there were even whole villages of us there.

I'd need some money. Figuring how to get it almost took my mind off of Patricia. Pa wasn't letting me babysit anymore because, he said, queers are child molesters. Who thinks up this shit? The only child I ever molested was Patricia, and I was a child myself at the time. Does that count?

But money. I studied all the possibilities, like that Mama might be sorry enough to give me some, and I decided my best bet was my sister Rayanne. She was too young to drive, but she was saving up for a car anyway. She thought ahead. She was making hamburgers at McDonald's, socking all her money away. Add that to years of babysitting money and berry-picking money, and — for a kid — she was loaded.

It was kind of hard to get her alone, with Pa watching and the house full of sisters, all real interested in me of course, wondering why Pa was so mad at me, wondering why I wasn't friends with Patricia anymore, watching and eavesdropping.

But one Saturday when Rayanne was raking leaves in the back yard, I had my chance.

"I've got to have some money," I said. There was no time to build up tactfully. "I've got to go to New York."

She was immediately full of love and worry. "What's the matter?" she asked.

"I can't tell you."

"You're pregnant!"

"I can't tell you."

"Listen, don't get an abortion. I'll help you. We'll go away. We'll raise the baby."

"I just have to go to New York. Don't ask me why."

"I'm coming too."

"No, I have to go alone."

Then Pa yelled, "Rayanne, you get in here!" and she had to go.

But the next Monday, I found an envelope with three hundred dollars' worth of twenty-dollar bills under my pillow. What a truly good person Rayanne always was. She came through for me like that, when I'd spent my whole life beating her away.

I left her a note saying I owed her three hundred dollars and a thousand backscratches and I would pay both debts before she was old enough to get a driver's license. At least the money part was true.

I jammed what clothes I could into my book bag and wore my winter jacket even though the day was warm, Indian summer. Instead of going to school, I caught the New York bus.

I thought back over how mean I'd always been to Rayanne. I made her ashamed to wear a swimsuit or short sleeves because her vaccination stuck out. I hid her doll and called in a squeaky little whine, "Rayanne! Rayanne! It's Dorothy! I'm lost! Save me!" Rayanne knew it was me, but she would run around crying anyway, looking for her doll. Rayanne loved the name Dorothy because it was Orothyday in Pig Latin. Why had I wanted to be mean to a little girl who thought Orothyday was the most beautiful word in the world? Why had I never taken my turn scratching her back? "You owe me eight hundred and fifty backscratches," she'd say while scratching mine. "Isn't that wonderful?" I'd say. "Just think of all the backscratches you're going to get!"

I had spent my life beating away her love, but here it was, good as new, and here was her life savings pinned in my pocket. Love, I saw, was something you don't have to deserve. In another few minutes I saw the bad part of that: love is something you *can't* deserve. Deserving Patricia's love didn't mean I was going to get it.

So, like always, Rayanne got shoved out of my head by Patricia.

I thought about New York, which I had never heard one good word for. "Dirty." "Dangerous." Those were the words. Crowded, expensive, cruel, greedy, cold-hearted. Queer. That was a good word, but the ones who said it meant it bad. "Scary." They'd as soon kill you as look at you. You can have a heart attack on the street and they'll just step right over you. Rich snots in limousines, bums sleeping on cardboard on the sidewalk, panhandlers who follow you and insult you if you don't give them money. Every bad thing I'd heard about New York came back. I was scared. My insides felt cold and hard as iron, but all the while I was also sweating, and not just from too many clothes. I began to think I wouldn't even be able to find Becky's mother.

The good part was, being scared wiped out Patricia. Whenever she crossed my mind, I switched to the evil roaring subway I'd probably get lost in, and she disappeared immediately.

One thing outlanders never hear about New Yorkers is how they like to help. I've found that over and over. If you have a camera or a map, so they're sure you're from out of town and won't beat them up for asking, you can't go ten steps without somebody saying, "Can I help you?" I didn't need a camera that day to look lost. I was lost when I stepped off the bus high up in that crazy snail shell of a bus station, and I kept on being lost while a whole long series of nice people pointed me to the escalator, onto the downtown subway, off it at what was labeled West Fourth Street but wasn't, and ended me up ringing the right doorbell of a tall skinny red-brick house on Perry Street. *Then* I wondered if I should have phoned first.

A woman called out, "Who is it?" I looked around and finally up, and there she was, leaning across a window box in the fourth-floor window. I like to remember that first look at Mother One. She had geraniums around her. Frost comes late in New York.

I yelled, "I'm a friend of Becky's."

I saw M-1 think *oh my God!* but she dropped me a string with a key on it. I let myself in and climbed the endless stairs. Another good word for New Yorkers: they're strong. They walk everywhere and climb stairs a lot.

M-1 was strong, and she was as tall as me. I'm not used to that. Our generation is supposed to be so tall, from all that right nutrition, but we're not, except me. I really liked her tallness and her face, which was sort of plain and grouchy, and her hair getting gray when it wanted to, not dyed.

I liked the apartment, too, but I hoped it didn't cost much. Even though it was the whole fourth floor, it was little, and I could see that the next room had no windows at all. But everything was comfortable and pretty, really a home. Instead of a TV set, there was a lit-up fish tank with tiny bright fish in it.

While M-1 was in the kitchen making us some tea, I sat and strained to see what was in the room that had no windows. I guessed it was probably the bedroom, the very bedroom. I could have made sure by pretending to look at a picture on the wall, but I was really afraid to see the bed and get overcome and make an ass of myself. I was afraid I might gasp or squeak or giggle. There was no knowing what the sight of a grown-up lesbian bed would do to me.

M-1 brought the tea and we sat sipping it, watching the fish. They weren't dashing around. They were peaceful. We didn't look at each other. M-1 was nervous. She told me the names of all the fish, zebra and neon and gourami and so on. She asked how I liked my school. (Fine.) Have the leaves been nice this fall? (Yes.) And when she couldn't think of one more thing to say to this strange schoolgirl that had fallen out of the sky, and we'd been quiet so long that I either had to say what I'd come to say or leave, I said, "Uh —"

More silence.

"Uh —"

"Umm?" she said.

"Uh — uh — what do you do when the one you love won't speak to you anymore?"

"So that's what you came all this way to ask me," she said. "I was hoping it might be something I had an answer to."

There went my last hope. The one grown-up who might have told me didn't know. Her breastbone must have hurt a lot when she was doing her housewife and mother number. And she must have done something about it or to it, because here she was, alive.

"I guess you forgot," I said, and hung my head. I was out of ideas.

"You want techniques?"

"Yes. Something to *do*."

"There are plenty of opinions. Some people say work hard. Hard physical work. Push wheelbarrows full of rocks uphill. Some people say read great literature. Once when I was down like that, I read Kierkegaard. *Fear and Trembling.* Couldn't put it down. Then my life took a better turn and next time I tried to read it I couldn't make head or tail of it. Are we talking about homosexuality?"

I said, "I guess so. It's a girl. We did everything."

"What happened?"

"I told my mother."

M-1 said, "Um." She saw the whole thing from that. I didn't have to spell out what a fool I'd been.

She said, "Some people recommend hard mental work. Learn a language. Learn a musical instrument. Learn physics. Some people recommend a kill-job. That's where you systematically deny every beauty you found with her. How do you think everybody you know got the way they are? They did kill-jobs. It's an awful way. It killed their hearts too. Some people say devote yourself to others, but they usually mean devote yourself to *them.* That's an awful way too."

M-2 came in then. She looked like a little plump mother dressed for church, except she had her necklace and earrings in her hand. She'd taken them off on the way upstairs.

M-1 said, "Hi, honey. This is Sharon. Her father used to be your oil man. We're thinking up ways to get over a girl."

M-2 glanced at me, not warmly, and went into the next room. "What would you know about that?" she yelled. "Lucille, come in here a minute, please."

They murmured, but I've got these really good ears. *Minor child,* I heard. "She's not asking for a solution." *Contributing to the delinquency of a minor. Hell of a mess.* "She's asking for acknowledgment."

From back home, yet! Are you crazy? "I can't bear for another generation to have nowhere to turn." *Shut up and let me handle this.*

They came back to the living room. M-2 was dressed in jeans, sweatshirt and sneakers. She said, "Young lady, if you think you have a problem, you should seek out a psychiatrist at once."

It really helped that M-1 stood behind her and grinned at me.

M-2 said, "Do your parents know where you are?"

"No."

"Phone them immediately. Not from here. And don't tell them where you've been. Tell them you were afraid to leave the bus station. When's your bus?"

"Uh — I don't know."

She phoned the bus station. "You have forty-five minutes," she told me. "We'll take you in a cab."

"Oh, that's okay. I'll find my way."

She saw through me. "I'll put you on the bus. I'll tell the driver you're a minor child. I'll tell him your father's meeting you. This your coat? This your schoolbag?"

We walked to Abingdon Square for a cab. Night was coming on. The city was looking a little weird, not necessarily something I wanted to be alone and homeless in. The bus station was even weirder. I saw that I was dumb and green and unprepared. I saw the M's really would get in trouble if they helped me. Who would believe they weren't child molesters, when my own father, who knew I wasn't, said I was?

I phoned home from a pay phone, collect. "I'm in New York. I've been in the bus station all day. I'm coming home."

"You damn right you are," Pa said.

M-1 said, "Sharon, in answer to your question. Make up your mind to bear it. Not to die. Not to go crazy. Just dig in and bear it. Get a good education. Go to college. Get a profession. Get ready to take care of yourself. Keep your heart alive. Love again."

I looked out the bus window at the Mothers standing there, tall and short like Patricia and me, soft and tough. M-2 untoughened a little, once she saw I was really leaving. She wiped her forehead and shook a flood of make-believe sweat off her hand. She came very near to smiling. She came very near to waving.

Strange to say, I was just as grateful to M-2 as to M-1 and loved them both the same.

CHAPTER FOUR:
Patricia

I couldn't understand why the shrink didn't say I was well and discharge me. I looked like a doll. I burbled about Mike. I saw several good qualities in my mother. My grades were respectable but not competitive. I looked to my father and brother for guidance and protection. I never mentioned Sharon. What magic healthy word had I not yet said? Or did the shrink just need the money?

Then one day he asked, "How do you feel about me?"

"You're very nice. Very patient with me," I said carefully. Wrong answer, I saw in his face.

Enough of being the only blindfolded player in this game. On my way home I stopped at the library and checked out four psychology books — Freud, Sullivan, Fromm-Reichmann, and Rogers. They were hard, heavy books, small print. I couldn't really read them, but every spare minute for weeks I skimmed them. I skipped the theory and went for the cases.

So *that* was it. I was supposed to love my shrink, that turkey! I was supposed to have a transference, a whole new neurosis. Therapy would consist in resolving it. We hadn't even begun. I just hoped my parents didn't know that.

Mother was sitting on the kitchen counter, watching the meatloaf bake and having a martini. Her martinis were getting bigger and bigger. This one filled a malted milk glass.

She didn't work on the house anymore. I overheard Daddy telling her a mother who scraped and painted and sawed and hammered was not a good feminine role model, and maybe my peculiarities were her fault.

I should say my *former* peculiarities. I had none by then. I was a clean slate.

I tried to think how a truly ordinary girl would talk to her mother. "Hi, Mother! What's for dinner? Meatloaf? Yum!"

"You're on thin ice, kid."

There was more gone from her glass than I'd thought. Maybe this wasn't a good time. On the other hand, if she was at the point of not remembering, I could tell her anything next day. She was always ashamed to admit she couldn't remember.

"Listen, Mother, what say I drop the shrink?"

"Oh no you don't! Don't you come at me when you know I'm non compos and try to get a far-reaching commitment out of me. Ask your father."

"Sure, I'll ask him too. I just wanted to know what you thought."

"I think it's a waste of money. You are you and always will be. You've got a steel neck and steel jaws and the sooner you drop this damn Betty Boop act, the better off we'll all be."

Everett could hide a cow in his nose and she wouldn't see it, but let me try to get away with one little bitsy fraud, *ever!* I could have killed her, but Truly Ordinary Girl merely wept and said, "Mother, you hurt me. Don't you know how hard I've tried? Don't you see how much I've changed?"

"In fact, I do."

"Isn't it enough?"

"It's enough. Drop the shrink. You can quote me. Now scram. I'm celebrating Michael's absence, having my drink in peace."

"You don't like Mike?" Truly Ordinary whined. Mike, the crown and proof of mental health? Those endless jeans, those huge sneakers, those armsful of records? "There's no pleasing you. You don't like anybody."

"I like Sharon," Mother said.

I was furious. Truly Ordinary disappeared, and red-haired Patricia yelled, "*Now* you tell me!"

"You didn't ask."

"You made me give her up."

"That wasn't me. Why would I? I'm not a real Burley. Burley Family disgraces roll right off me."

I'd forgotten this was all about being a Burley. Was I going to have to get a transference after all?

"Sharon's a good kid," Mother said. "She's smart. She's alive. She has no affectations. She has a modest, unadorned human face. She's brave. She doesn't let anybody tell her not to know what she knows."

"You're so unfair! You like her better than me!"

"No I don't," Mother said.

"Yes you do, and you're drunk, and you always will be. You're a destroyed person."

Mother set her big glass down and came over to me and took my arm and twisted me to the floor. She pinned me down with all her soft weight and held both my wrists in one hand. I had never noticed she was strong. I caught the web of her thumb in my teeth and chomped down hard. She didn't notice. With her free hand she made little half-chops at my head, not touching it, saying, "If you move a muscle I'll break you to bits. I am not destroyed. I am suffering. There's a difference. I hope you never know why I drink. I hope life never gets that bad for you. I like Sharon because she loves her mother. You have always been my enemy. You called the food I cooked you garbage. You wouldn't clean the room I made pretty for you. You never said a simple friendly word to me. You've always been my enemy. I hate you."

Then she let me up and we both cried, I loudly because I'd read that silent crying does no good, and she silently. She turned off the oven and went up to her room. I went to mine, still howling in order to get the benefits of howling, but inside really peaceful.

Even though every one of her charges was true, I knew she forgave me. I don't think I'd have done all those things to hurt her feelings if I had imagined I could. I always thought I was too unimportant to her to be able to hurt her. I mean, I never thought a girl could hurt her. Remembering how gently she pretended to beat my head, how carefully she missed me, I knew she loved me. And I knew she wouldn't remember anything.

But next morning as I was making my breakfast, she rushed in, saying, "Patricia, did I say I've always hated you?"

"No," I said. I felt so calm and sweet and loved. "You said, 'You've always been my enemy. I hate you.'"

She let out a long, relieved breath.

I asked, "How's your hand?"

"My hand?"

"I bit you."

"You did?"

"Yup."

Somehow our fight, with all its dangers of estranging Mother and me forever, had washed the poison out of us. She looked at the red curve of broken skin my teeth had left and laughed and shook her head. I brought a gauze square and tape and covered her wound so Daddy wouldn't ask about it. We forgot about first-aid spray.

But she laughed even when the bite got infected. "How sharper than a serpent's tooth is a thankless child's tooth," she said.

And I — I felt as proud as though I'd got her pregnant.

* * * * *

So at last I saw that Mother was wonderful, but I got impatient with her soon again. Why, for instance, being wonderful, had she let Daddy take her away from a professorship at Vassar and make a servant of her? Did she *like* being Siamese twin to an ironing board while the rest of the world went drip-dry? Was she really amused when Daddy or Everett held up an unironed handkerchief and said, cutely-archly, "Chief Hanker hankers for one minute of your time?" Why did she look guilty the one time Daddy swept up a light bulb he'd broken, as though a male shouldn't have to sweep? It's true he gave her a reproachful look, but couldn't she have laughed at him? Did she have to share his solemn view of himself? Why did she go to the Old Place, since, weirdly, she didn't like it? A whole lot of her life went down the drain there, for nothing.

I appointed myself Mother's defender. I felt, in fact, she'd chosen me, that she was counting on me. (All right, I admit the shrink made me see I felt that, and made me see I was proud of it.) The trouble was, I didn't want to fight with Daddy about how he treated her, or show any indignation about women's lot in the world, because I wanted him to think I was normal and ready to drop the shrink. So my protection took the form of urging Mother to protect herself. I do think I was taking hold of the right end, besides taking care of myself. What good does it do to open the cage if the bird won't fly? First convince the bird it's a prisoner, *then* open the cage. Smart as she was, capable as she was, Mother wouldn't be

convinced and my protection came to nothing. She
said I didn't understand. I sure didn't.

Well, I knew *I* was a prisoner, anyway, and I
knew who had the key to my cage. Daddy had always
been a pushover for me — a few girlish giggles and
pouts got me whatever I wanted. He never understood
why Mother found such a sweet little kid so
formidable. But ever since this hassle about Sharon
started, he'd been strange. Sort of serious and
awkward. Embarrassed. After making me laugh all my
life, he started saying dumb things like, "How are
you, Patricia?" Hollowly, and gazing, waiting for an
answer. He patted my hair and shoulder sometimes,
as though he'd resolved to be affectionate. As though
I went bad because he wasn't warm enough. So I was
embarrassed too, but I knew I had to treat him as I
always had and get us back to our old easy footing
and be declared well.

He was reading in the living room, wearing his
old car-washing pants split in both legs. His pudgy
knees stuck out and I went up, exactly like a
confident beloved child, and tickled them, saying,
"Wouldn't the State Board of Agriculture be pleased
if they knew professors wear out their pants at the
knees? Wouldn't they give the university a lot of
money?" I kissed his shiny bald head, that amazingly
smooth skin, almost as good as a breast except hard
inside, and sat on the arm of his chair.

"You're not doing summer school, are you? We
can go to the Old Place?" I said.

"Well, uh, I haven't decided about the Old Place. I do need to touch base again, but, uh, I wouldn't want to interrupt your therapy."

"Oh, pooh on my therapy. Let's go!"

"Well, it's very uh important. We want to give you the best possible start in life."

"*Pooh* on therapy. It's silly. The Old Place is my good start in life."

"Well, uh, I've been considering leaving you and your mother here —"

"Daddy!"

"Please hear me out." That was his quaint way of saying shut up and listen. "I'm sure you agree that it wouldn't be fair to deprive Everett of the Old Place on your account."

"I *don't* agree. Why deprive *any*body? Why deprive Mother and me?"

"I think she wouldn't experience it as deprivation."

"Well *I* would."

He got up and walked around. I slid down into his warm chair.

"Uh, Patricia, I don't know how to put this," he said. "But there's, uh, an unwritten code, not to take anything unsuitable to the Old Place."

"I'm suitable!"

"If you had a, uh, communicable disease — if *one* did — one would naturally not expose the family to it. That's just basic decency."

"But I'm well! I'm well! Can't you see?"

"Physically. But, frankly, I've been waiting for some sign that you understand the seriousness — the magnitude — of this uh business with Sharon."

"We were *playing*."

"Once again, you're making light of it. Well, I have a class to get ready for. We can continue this later if you like. I'm open to persuasion. I'm eager to be persuaded. Let me see a serious grappling with a serious problem," he said.

He was completely out of my control.

I couldn't figure out a way to seem to grapple any better than I had, and Daddy and Everett went to the Old Place without Mother and me. Since lolling around with Mike hadn't impressed anybody, I told him I wanted to spend a lot of time with Mother and get to know her. He knew I was lying, but he obediently wandered off. He had better things to do during a sexual revolution than get his T-shirt sucked.

I mostly stayed in my room, drawing pictures of the Old Place from memory and snapshots, and being serious about the fun I was missing, but pretty soon I did begin to enjoy being alone with Mother. I hadn't known what a strain men were.

We had an easy summer of TV dinners and Kleenex and the flowers she finally had a chance to raise. We even went to McDonald's. Sometimes we had oatmeal and hard-boiled eggs for supper and I'd say, "Just what I always wanted — a good breakfast!" Mother rented a TV set and many nights we sat up watching that gray flicker until our eyes turned tiny and red. Other nights she worked on her pitiful ambition to be organized by going through her

papers — a lifetime's mess of letters, abandoned
manuscripts, junk mail, clippings, recipes. She'd be
reading and deciding, filing or throwing away, and I'd
sit on the daybed behind her playing my guitar and
singing my little repertoire — "Shorty George,"
"East Virginia," "O Lula!" and our favorite, "I Got
No Use for Women," which always made us laugh.

Not being tragic felt so good that I began to get
less mad at Sharon too. That was my summer to
forgive female dumbness. I decided to tell Sharon
everything would be okay in a couple of years when
we grew up, and just hang in there.

The problem was how to get past that massive
father of hers. He wasn't even letting her outdoors,
and I never saw her silhouetted in the dark watching
my window any more. I figured he'd moved her bed
to a back room.

Sharon's sister Rayanne worked at McDonald's, so
I wrote Sharon a note and carried it in my shorts
pocket to be ready when my chance came to ask
Rayanne to give it to Sharon. The note was very
scuffed-up and smudgy by the time Mother asked me
to go alone to McDonald's on my bike, but at last
there I was at the head of the line face to face with
Rayanne, holding out my soggy paper pellet and
saying, "Slip this to Sharon somehow, please."

"She's gone," Rayanne said.

"Gone? Where?"

"Pa took her to Grandma's."

"Where's Grandma's?"

Before Rayanne could answer, the manager came
over. "Are you ready to place your order? Others are
waiting."

I was too upset to care "Where?" I yelled.
"Rayanne can socialize on her own time."
"Two burgers, two large fries. *Where?*"
"Pa told us not to tell you," Rayanne said.

CHAPTER FIVE:
Sharon

What made Pa think his mother would be a good keeper for me? Maybe while he was growing up in that farmhouse full of big loud men, he hadn't bothered to notice her. She must have had some quirks all along. You can't tell me she became a full-time kook just like *that*, overnight, when Grandpa died.

I didn't care, myself, where I went, as long as it was away from the danger of seeing Patricia with

Mike. I bitched to Pa a little about how the nearest town, Mote, was invisible — a general store with a gas pump out front, a grain elevator, a milk station, a diner, a school, a church — to make him feel he was really tough, really punishing me, but I truly didn't care.

The joke was on Pa. He wanted for me to feel like hell at Grandma's and see what happens to you when you're funny, but what he got was me being, all in all, in the end, thankful.

When we drove up, Grandma was on the roof in her overalls. We hardly saw that the yard was full of concrete statues of dwarfs in groups of seven, and animals and birds and frogs and mushrooms and Virgin Marys. Grandma up on the roof was what we saw.

"You'll break your fool neck!" Pa yelled.

"No I won't," she said and climbed neatly down her ladder. She looked pretty good, big and soft but probably brittle inside. Why was she doing all this work anyway, when she was just going to die and never get the good of it?

"Sharon," she said, "you went and got tall."

Pa said, "That's not the half of what she went and got. I want you to ride pretty tight herd on her."

"Sure will," she said, turning her head to hide one eye from him. She winked at me straight-faced with it.

She sent me into the house to pick out a bedroom, she didn't care which. There were five to choose among, that smelled hot and dusty like attics and echoed like caves. I didn't like any of them, but chose one that looked down on an apple tree full of tiny unround green apples, and went back downstairs to get some sheets for the iron bed, that some big loud uncle had grown up in.

Pa was already leaving. He didn't like to drive at night, especially in the mountains. Grandma didn't offer to feed him. "Goodbye, Ivan," she said. "Thanks for bringing Sharon. Give everybody my best." He looked sort of puzzled when he drove away. I think he thought mothers were supposed to have a passion to feed people, and feel all lost when their family grew up, and cling to sons when visits were over.

"Well, Sharon, how are you on heights?" she asked.

"I don't know."

"You'll soon find out. We'll start you on the low part."

I worked at prying rotten shingles off the kitchen wing, getting used to the height, that sicky rush. One story is higher than it looks from the ground. Grandma was hauling up bundles of bright new cedar shingles on a pulley she'd rigged up.

"What did you do to get yourself banished?" she asked. "Dope? A boy?"

"No."

She let it drop, didn't push me, went on with her pulley. I practiced standing up without freaking out.

That night in a vision Grandma saw a clear, pure stream of water. "That's your soul, pure and clear and clean," she said next day. "The vision was sent to tell me I can teach you. You won't interfere, and you won't put the knowledge to an evil use."

For instance, she told me cars and tractors were invented because horses suffered so much during the Napoleonic Wars and worked off all their karma. What do you do with that?

She said she used to wonder and wonder about Nevada. She didn't believe in divorce any more than she believed in marriage. What had Nevada done to deserve all that divorce and nuclear testing and gambling? Then she found out there'd been a massacre there and she had her answer. Nevada would suffer till it paid off the karma for that massacre.

Not the kind of knowledge you can get rich in the witch-doctor business with. But she also taught me to drive a nail straight and snap a chalkline to lay a neat row of shingles.

She had a dozen projects, most of them heavy and hard, like those statues in the yard. "My beasts," she called them. She made them. Herself. And sold them to people on their way to somewhere else. So I learned to run a cement mixer and put armatures in the right places. She bought the molds. I schlepped many a fifty-pound bag of cement or sand, many a bundle of armatures. Before I came, she did all that alone. At last she trusted me to pour. That's not easy either. You can't stop once you start, have to keep an even flow, and at the same time you have to keep ramming the wet cement with a stick so there won't be any voids, but we always had voids anyway. Then when you unmold you have to patch the voids with mortar mix, and rasp off the mold lines. To me the beasts looked best just plain and gray, but they sold best painted. I liked making the Virgin Marys's dresses blue.

There were signs out front, boards nailed to stakes. DANICA ALMO, one said. LAWN ORNAMENTS took two boards. So did ORGANIC VEGETABLES. PLEASE

HONK fit on one. She'd taken down the weirdest ones before Pa could see them. I helped her put them back up. PSYCHIC READINGS. LOST OBJECTS. She had prayed that that wasn't a wrong use of her gift, and the Universe had said it understood, she had to make a living, didn't she? PIN CUSHIONS. DOLL FURNITURE. HEALING TOUCH. CUT FLOWERS.

The huge garden was mulched with straw and leaves so it didn't need weeding or watering. It did need more straw and leaves, though, as the underside turned to humus, and I was out there night and day, it felt like, hauling wheelbarrowsful. It also needed its slug traps baited with home-brew beer. The mulch was slug heaven.

I'm not sure mulching was easier than watering and weeding would have been, but the vegetables were great. Peas, carrots, radishes, string beans, then corn and tomatoes, really fresh, really ripe, really good — I suppose. We personally never ate any except tomatoes, which we bit holes in and sucked the insides out of. They spoiled me for store-bought tomatoes forever.

Grandma was through with cooking, except one big potful of goulash or chili on Sunday, that we chewed on all week. Cooking was work she could hide in the house on Sunday and not be accused of Sabbath-breaking, unlike roofing. "A witch can't be too careful," she said.

She didn't let me see her do her witch stuff, her psychic readings and visions of where lost objects went. For those, she wore a housedress and a flowered bib-apron. When people came — and some came every week, like to a shrink — she took them into the little room she kept locked and the curtains closed so I couldn't see in from the outside either.

Some days she would fast and in the evening shower again and put on a clean white cotton robe with no metal on it — no snaps, no zippers, no pins — and pretty soon I'd hear her talking sing-song and a thick sicky-sweet black smoke would come oozing through the door cracks and the curtains. That was frankincense being burned on consecrated charcoal, she told me. She said the Roman Catholic ritual was very good theurgically, whatever that meant, but didn't work anymore because the priests' robes were too thick with embroidery to be washed, and full of metal — gold. Their holy water still worked, though, if you knew how.

In winter we lived mostly in the kitchen where the woodstove kept us warm. The rest of the house had little ridges of snow on the windowsills. Old farm houses were never built to be heated. They weren't even insulated. You stayed by the stove, and at bedtime you took your brick that had been heating all day on the stove and wrapped it thick with newspapers and put it in your bed, which was deep in quilts, and jumped in fast. You touched the brick with your toe but it was too hot, and again and again, but still too hot, and by the time you could cuddle it between your feet you were asleep, sad or not. The smell of hot newspapers really touches me, really chokes me up.

The kitchen, Grandma told me, was the original log cabin plastered over and sided over and added onto when the pioneer family got prosperous. It was hard to believe that poor old house, creaking its way

back to the ground and paintless like driftwood, ever
meant somebody was prosperous, but Grandma said
yes, it was really very grand, a showplace once.
Before her time, of course. And the heart of it was
the log-cabin kitchen, where we sat at a round oak
table five feet across with a light bulb hanging down
above it, and she made stuff and I studied or made
stuff.

She'd sit at the table with tin-cutting shears, like
a more or less ordinary person (I mean, not like a
witch), snipping coffee cans into thin strips still
attached to the can bottom. With needle-nosed pliers,
she'd bend half the strips down and twist them
together to be fancy little legs, and half up to be a
fancy twisted back. She'd gold-paint it all. She'd pad
the can bottom into a seat, and presto! a pin cushion
in the shape of an elegant ballroom chair.
Razor-sharp, of course, but really cute from a safe
distance.

She didn't care about cute. She did nothing except
for money, including giving me houseroom. Pa had to
pay. Nothing was play with her, and yet in a way
everything was play. The game was called Taking
Care of Myself, and she was slowly losing it. Not
enough time. Not enough hands, even with my two
good ones added. Every year she had to sell a little
more land, another houselot, in order to pay taxes
and break even. The farm was down to thirty acres
— the wrecky barn and sheds, the huge garden,
hayfields and pasture that she leased to the
neighbors, and a mixed beech and maple woodlot. She
was hoping to die before the woodlot had to go.

Those pincushions had a small but hot market.
Otherwise she wouldn't have made them. But it was

land that had paid to bring in the powerline and pipe
in water for a flush toilet and a hot shower, which
Grandpa always said was silly sissy stuff nobody
really needed. If he hadn't been already dead, he'd
have croaked when she sold his fields for that. But
I'm on her side.

What everybody liked was the doll furniture. Even
I did. We could hardly keep it in stock. We cut it out
of thin balsa sheets with X-Acto knives and glued it
together and stained it and varnished it, tiny dressers
with drawers that worked and tables and chairs and
beds, grandfather clocks. It wasn't for children. It was
to remind grownups of the family things they'd
thrown away.

One morning Grandma said, "Something is
guiding me to make a log cabin."

I was as money-minded as her by then, and I said,
"But it won't sell."

"Maybe it's not supposed to sell. You just take
the pruning shears and go cut me some nice half-inch
maple branches."

To show her how dumb and unbusinesslike she
was being, I brought her a whole maple limb and
dumped it on the porch. She didn't care. She set to
with the pruning shears cutting twelve-inch and
twenty-inch lengths. She said, "Now go get me some
little flat stones for the fireplace and chimney, little
chips of slate would be just right."

Here we were just barely keeping up with the doll
furniture, and I was picking up stones. I took my
time and was none too choosy. When I came back
with a bagful of stones I knew were mostly too big,
she had six courses of tiny logs laid up and was

notching some more. There was a little doorway. Two windows. I looked at it and began to cry.

She pretended she didn't notice. "I'm giving it a lift-off roof. It has to have a bed with a pretty quilt. Tree of Life, I think. I can fake it with crayons."

I just kept on crying. I didn't know why. Because I couldn't go home? Something about home. I didn't know what.

"It was a girl," I heard myself say.

"I was one of those once," Grandma said. I guessed I couldn't blame her for being out-of-it, when she didn't even know what question I was answering.

"I mean, a queer," she said, whittling away at her notch, neat and steady.

I just looked at that little cabin home and kept on crying. Who could know what an old lady like that might mean by "queer?" Maybe she meant she didn't like strawberries or something.

"Not in this life, of course," she said. "I know how to go back and take a peek. Don't tell your dad."

I said, "Don't worry. Then he'd lock us both up."

She said, "I've been a big black African chief. I've been lots of things. And once I was a preacher that got unfrocked for making my congregation laugh during prayer. For laughter they condemned me. What would they have done if they knew I liked the boys! But I escaped and became a traveling bookseller. America was perishing in darkness then, just like now. Things don't get worse. Don't let 'em kid you."

She finished her log, put it in place, and stood back to admire. "I know now," she said, "that it's hard to be white and hard to be black and hard to be a man and hard to be a woman, but back then I thought being white and a woman would be easy. I thought I wanted to be simple. I thought all I wanted was to take care of some good man and make him a baby every year." She sighed. "It was a natural mistake."

"Pa thinks I'm really bad," I said, crying again.

She said, "He thinks no such thing. He's trying to save you from other people."

"What could other people do that he didn't do?"

"Be that as it may, that's his intention."

"He acts like he hates me."

"He doesn't hate you. You broke a rule, that's all. He's showing you what it costs to break a rule."

"Is there a rule to not love your friend?"

"No, no. Come on, I'm going to show you something."

She unlocked her secret room with the key she carried around her neck on a string, and carefully opened the door. "Better take off your shoes," she said. "It's a little bit holy. Medium holy."

I took off my shoes and followed her in. The room was dark, but she opened the curtains and the bright sunlight came in.

She said, "Look around all you want — you won't understand anything."

I understood so little I couldn't even remember what all was there. I remembered a bright-colored chart with circles on stems, like a lollipop tree, and a wooden table with some wooden boxes and a double candle holder on it, and the smell of frankincense. Everything was very clean. A bare wooden floor, white walls. A wooden box with earth in it. The room had a little bit of an echo from being practically empty, but echo or not, it was plain and bright and unspooky. I suspected Grandma's sewing machine might be tucked away somewhere.

"Look at this," Grandma said, pointing to a cross on the wall. It wasn't like a Jesus cross. All four arms were the same size, with three lobes on the ends like clover leaves. "See what it says," she said.

I went up close and read.

"Read it out loud," she said.

I read the top arm: " 'To dare.' "

"Go on."

I had to bend my head to the side to read, " 'To will.' "

"Go on."

I bent my head the other way and said, " 'To know.' "

"Go on."

I practically stood on my head and slowly figured out the upside-down words. " 'To remain silent.' "

"There you have the rule you broke."

The advice had a sort of official feel to it, coming off of a cross like that, in a secret room like that. It was like a command, and really discouraging. Here I was living in a house too shabby to invite anybody to, and a stranger in a new high school, which was hard and lonesome enough by itself, without being commanded to remain silent. How was I going to get to know anybody if I didn't let anybody know me? Was I supposed to stay by myself all day and then hurry away after school, like some poor soul mainstreamed from a mental hospital?

* * * * *

At graduation all the other kids ran around crying
and saying the happiest part of their life was over,
but I knew life had to get better than that or why
bother?

I don't mean high school was all bad. Grandma
kind of turned me on to learning. She said
everything's interesting if you take hold of it right,
and you can get a decent education even in Mote
Consolidated High School if you pay attention.
"Remember what else the cross told you: 'To
Know.' "

So I learned how to drive in driver education,
though all I had to practice on was Grandma's awful
old truck Papa Bear. And how to bisect an angle and
type forty words a minute and read a map and speak
and write, more or less, my native language — that's
just minimum, Grandma said — and a few other
things like that, that probably weren't what the cross
meant at all. But I was so lonesome, lonesome to the
bone. I was such an outsider.

I used to climb the hill north of the house and
watch the sunset until the first star came out, and
wish on it and walk down to supper in the
almost-dark. That star, which was not a star but the
planet Venus, was my only friend. With it, I didn't
have to Remain Silent. I asked it to let me be,
someday, not lonesome.

I was the first one in my family to get, ever, a
high school diploma. All my folks, down to the
youngest sister, came to my graduation. I was really
glad to see them. They looked so nice, so handsome,
every single one, sitting in a row on folding chairs in
the gym. All Mote could see that I wasn't just some
weirdo outcast who lived in an unpainted house, but

an honored member of a solid, good-looking, well-dressed family. Well-dressed would count most.

I was valedictorian. You just about can't help being if you pay attention. So I had to give a speech. "Valedictorian" turned out to mean "The One Who Says Goodbye." I got through it all right. Even though I saw by the way Grandma was working her mouth that she couldn't wait to take her lower teeth out, I didn't laugh.

Back at the house afterwards, Pa said, "Well, Sharon, you looked pretty good up there, and you didn't sound any worse than the rest of them. I wasn't ashamed of you."

I think that was the first praise he ever gave me, and almost more than I could handle. It didn't even make me feel good. Embarrassed, was what I felt.

He said, "So what comes next?"

"Could I maybe go to college?"

"I guess you can go anyplace now. You can be as fancy as you please. You're a grown woman now. You're on your own."

Yes, I was a grown woman and I was a child too. But what else could I expect from somebody who hadn't even wanted to pay for my kindergarten?

Mama said, "Ivan, she needs a profession. She needs something to fall back on in case her husband dies or something."

Sweet Mama. I did wish she knew how to manage him better. At least she tried.

"Husband! She's the one that'll be the husband!"

I could see my sisters trying to figure that one out.

Grandma said, "Why, Ivan, what a thing to say about your own child, who made us all so proud tonight! Such a dear girl, just as quick and hardworking as can be."

Grandma was pretty good at her Kindly Granny number. She'd even kept her teeth in, to be cuter, for all the good it did. To Pa, education was a fancy waste of time. Even high school was fancy. He'd done all right without it, hadn't he? And you don't need school to do woman things.

There was just no way he was going to help me. The money he gave Grandma for my keep would stop too. She wouldn't be able to afford me long without it.

My folks drove home that night. Before they left, Mama got me alone a minute and gave me some money. She put her fingers over my lips to keep me quiet and put this wad of bills in my pocket. I tried to give it back, because I knew it was her secret life savings, the little pennies she'd told Pa she'd spent on groceries but hadn't, for years. She got tears in her eyes and shook her head, and I knew she was saying she was sorry she'd tattled on me and made my life so sad, so I kept the money. It turned out to be seven hundred and fifty dollars, enough to go to New York on, I hoped.

I stayed on with Grandma, to help her get the garden in, and to write a letter to Mother One. I knew she wouldn't send an answer to my father's house.

"I'm eighteen now. You can talk to me," I wrote. "I took your advice. I made up my mind not to die or go crazy. I'm through school. If I lived in New York would I ever see you?"

I knew she'd remember me. I knew there was nobody else like me in her life. "I can't bear for another generation to have nowhere to turn," she had said. I knew she'd answer me.

While I waited for her letter, I hauled mulch. I set out tomato plants on the south-facing slope, each in its paper collar. Grandma could still bend over but not kneel, and if she sat on the ground it was in doubt she could get back up.

She had taught me Healing Touch, which is feeling for a hurty place and holding it with your thumb for seven seconds and then letting up slowly and moving on an inch at a time until you find another hurty place to hold. "Anything that hurts is asking to be held," she said. Healing Touch really works, and people don't have to take their clothes off and feel silly or make you feel silly. I could fix up Grandma, but then she'd wreck herself again the next day. I worried what would happen to her when I left.

Mother One's letter was so careful, so nothing, that I figured she'd had to fight with Mother Two to write it at all, and her handwriting was awful. "Thanks for your note. We're busy and happy here. The weather is lovely. Do stay in touch." She could have put it on a postcard. It thrilled me like a love letter. I couldn't stop rereading it.

Grandma said I should answer Mother One with a list of all I could do, for her to show her friends in case one of them could give me a job in their store or office or cleaning their house or walking their dog or something — anything. I was sort of encouraged by how long my list was. Then Grandma read it and reminded me of a few things more, and she made me tell I was valedictorian, too. How embarrassing! I'm willing to brag, but not about Mote Consolidated High School.

"So they'll see you can learn. So they'll see you're promising," Grandma said. I like to remember that. It helps me not give up on myself in dumb times.

Everything I owned — including a copy of Grandma's cross she made for me — fit with room to spare into a backpack. There was a bus that came through Mote once a week, just often enough to keep its franchise in case the company wanted it later. Grandma and I stood by the highway. She waved the bus to stop, and away I went, scared and excited, a child and a grown woman both. Being excited made me see I'd been in creeper gear for a long time. Depressed, in fact. I don't want to put Grandma down. Being with her had its moments. But depressed is the right word. The finest grandmother in the world, which I suspect she was, couldn't make up for Mote.

I'd reserved a room at a poor grungy old hotel, not very clean, that smelled of bug spray, named the Abbey Victoria. It was at 51st Street and Seventh Avenue, right in the middle of midtown, and cheap — for New York. Grandma had stayed there once, when she appeared on *What's My Line* and stumped everybody. (The answer was witch. Luckily nobody in Mote could pick up that channel.)

The Abbey Victoria was crawling with kids with backpacks. I looked like them, but they were on their way to Europe on standby flights, just pausing to take a look at New York. If one of them had asked me, I'd have gone too. I hated feeling stodgy and

careful, old before my time, a granny, when I should
have belonged to my own generation, running to
catch a plane as its door was closing, ready to blow
all my money and trust to luck like them.

But nobody asked me, and I bought the papers
and some city maps and started looking for a job and
a room. I was determined not to bother the Mothers
until I was settled in and working, so I could be a
friend, not a problem.

The subway really mixed me up. I thought it was
one subway. Otherwise why did they call it *the*? I
thought it went round and round down here, like a
toy train on an oval track, and you could get on it
anywhere and sooner or later it would bring you to
every station. That's why I found Far Rockaway
while looking for the Lower East Side, but I studied
my maps and figured things out a little at a time.

I got a job as a printer's messenger. I carried copy
from stores and offices to the printer, and proofs and
repros and blueprints back again, before I knew the
city, while I was still getting lost. Even if I got off at
the right station, I'd still come up out of the tunnel
completely turned around, not knowing uptown from
downtown. I bought a dimestore compass to carry in
my pocket, but the needle pointed every which way. I
blamed the compass then, but later I found out all
compasses, and watches too, go crazy near me. I'm
kind of proud of being that magnetic, but it's a
nuisance.

New York gave me a lot of shocks at first. Such
as lambs with their wool still on hanging in butcher
shop windows. Such as blood in the gutters on
Gansevoort Street. Such as steam pouring out of

pipes in the street like leaks from hell. Such as men suddenly walking with me when I hadn't even looked at them and saying, "Hey, baby, you want a blow job?" That was when I wore a dress. Later when I cut my hair and wore jeans everywhere, they just called me dyke and passed me by. I have to wonder if enough straight women said yes to keep the men at it. Was it a sincere come-on? Did it work sometimes? Otherwise, why did they stop when they figured I wouldn't be interested?

And there were plenty of lower-level shocks, more like surprises, because I expected everything to be huger and grander than back home. But how like a bunch of old-timey hick towns New York was, a different one at each subway stop — dinky grocery stores you'd swear couldn't feed all those people, boys on big tricycles making deliveries, antique dealers kneeling on the sidewalk to refinish furniture because they had no room inside, lots of horse manure and dog turds, a cat in every window, men riding the subway train with fishpoles, going fishing.

And crowds, like university football crowds back home, but every day. At rush hour, New York sidewalks were as full as the streets, so full you had to stop and wait, couldn't hurry. On the trains and buses you were pushed against other people so tight you could have died and not fallen, and even if it wasn't rush hour, there was always somebody.

I remembered a line from a poem I'd learned in school. It was about London at dawn, and it went, "All that mighty heart is lying still." I kept trying to catch New York's mighty heart lying still, but it never was. Even at dawn somebody was walking around or a taxi was coming up the avenue. At its quietest, New York always had some kind of noise, at least a hum. You could feel it in your feet. Some people said it was just the subway trains rumbling along in their burrows at all hours, or air conditioners, but according to Grandma that hum came from the great cosmic force lines that intersect in New York, the focus of universal energy, and I believe her.

I loved being part of that energy. I loved walking every inch of New York on real errands, in all kinds of weather, with my canvas pouch and my yellow stomping boots. Whenever I saw a roomful of dressed-up typists, partly I'd feel sorry for them, and partly I'd think ha ha on you!

BOOK TWO

BOOK TWO

CHAPTER ONE:
Patricia

When it was time for college, I asked to go to Smith, as Mother had, but Daddy, in a pitifully white black accent, cried, "Oh, do throw me into de briar patch! Ah wants de briar patch!" My years of blameless living had not dimmed his memory of my crimes. Historians are like that.

He sent me to Brundidge-Willson College. He could have done worse. He could have sent me to a Bible college guaranteed to return me in four years with a full understanding of God's rage at us and an intact maidenhead, but luckily he was agnostic. The real danger was that he'd keep me at home and I'd be riding with him to the university every morning, like going to high school, when everybody knows the whole point of going to college is to leave town. Luckily he was a snob. The Burley Family did not send its children to large state-supported institutions with football teams.

I tried not to love Brundidge-Willson because it was so deliberately lovable — small and simple, maples and ivy, a waterfall — but I couldn't stop myself. The administration building was an old Shaker barn built of granite blocks. Nobody dressed up. The only athletes, the tennis team, carried their racquets in black cardboard suitcases to avoid detection. The president was a woman. She was said to make her own clothes and cut her own hair.

There was a nice mix of men and women, Daddy's foremost requirement, none of your monosexual hotbeds. Plenty of gentle, arrogant young men, but on my first day in English class I fell in love with the teacher, Ms. Hayes. So Daddy was right about me after all.

God, it felt good to sit there and love Ms. Hayes, whose name was Noel — the fall of her long shiny brown hair, her big round glasses, her square gappy teeth, her crazy accents (a touch of Oklahoma, a touch of Oxford) — and not resist, not regret, just let love pour, just let my heart and brain wake up.

"Born and bred in de briar patch, Daddy," I thought.

* * * * *

Noel Hayes was married to a black African with one of those wonderful black African names you wish you had thought up, Bassikounou. Everybody called him B. "We never meant to afflict our *relationship* with anything so dreary as *marriage*," she told me, "but it was the only way to get him into the goddamn *country*."

They were happy, like children, like Sharon and me before the shit came down. I'd see Noel rushing to hug B after class and away they'd go, holding hands and laughing. Sometimes, jabbering in his native tongue, he'd lop her over his shoulder and run off while she screamed, "Help! This savage is abducting me! Racial purity is threatened!"

So I knew my love was never going to be, as they say, consummated, but that wasn't the main thing. The main thing was that loving her brought back my old urge to be excellent. As good as a kiss was getting back a paper with a tiny "Nice" or "OK!" beside the title. I worked hard and made it happen a lot.

Every few days, Noel announced a march or rally. She was for abortion, marijuana, the end of curfew for women students, the unionization of clerical workers, liberalized immigration policies, and black civil rights — none of which had ever seemed to have anything to do with me, but I marched. Sometimes the whole march was just the two of us holding up signs and yelling. I felt really foolish at first, but some of Noel's bravery and sturdiness rubbed off on me a little at a time. I came to enjoy crying in the wilderness, being Horatio at the bridge. The best was afterward, when she'd take me home with her and give me horrible tea that tasted like smoked dirty socks, Lapsang Souchong, and tell me about holding America to its goddamn *promise*. B would be at the sewing machine making African pants and shirts, shogatos and dashikis. That was how he made his living.

Their apartment was one room, share the bath down the hall. "The only thing we could *get* in this racist *society*," Noel said. I loved the place. They had furnished it with junk from the street and made it beautiful. Every wall from floor to ceiling had crate shelves holding books and dishes and cardboard boxes decorated with collages appropriate to the contents. The box of linens, for instance, had a linen-spinning wheel. There was a sink in the corner, a chugging old refrigerator behind a curtain in a closet. The bed-couch-social center was a mattress on the floor, not very soft but handsomely covered with a throw B had pieced together out of his bright scraps. Quilts, neatly folded, were in a huge basket. On a board supported by two crates was Noel's Royal portable typewriter. She was writing a book.

"What about?" I asked.

"Never ask a writer that," she said. "If I could say it in two sentences — or ten — I wouldn't need to *write* it."

I felt so dumb. "Sorry," I said.

She said, "It's about men's belief that women are evil. That men would be angels if women weren't holding them by the *ankles*, dragging them back from the stars. That women epitomize all yin — you know about yin and yang?"

"Umm," I lied.

"That everything heavy, lightless, negative, tarry, sticky, dank, swampy, nasty, is *feminine*, is *yin*."

"They think that?"

"I'm accumulating a dossier. I'm getting the goods on them. *Yes* they think that. It's in their books, their philosophies, their religions. It's in *B*. Here he's off his turf. Prince Bassikounou's not pussy-whipped in *Africa,* you can bet."

"Does my father think I'm all that bad stuff?"

"That very question is what got me started. Why doesn't some President with daughters and no sons — Johnson, *Nixon* — stand up and scream, "Goddamn it, nobody can tell my *my child* is inferior!? Why didn't Henry the Eighth? Why don't men insist, if only out of pride, that their life-mates are, by God, *equal?* Who wants to mate with somebody who's not equal? What good is the love of a slave? Why have they always oppressed us?"

"Have you figured it out?" I asked.

"Why haven't they seen that it's in their interest as well as ours for us to be as strong and smart and capable as possible?"

"Why? I mean, why haven't they?"

"It's a great mystery. It's something to do with yin and yang. It's in the very structure of their psyches, I sometimes fear. Archetypal, I sometimes fear. That would make it ineradicable. The belief that if they can lock us up tight enough, bury us deep enough, *they can get rid of all the evil in the world.*"

I said, "But that's stupid! They're sort of awful, but they're not stupid."

"No, thank God," Noel said. "So I'm hoping if I can show them they believe a stupid thing they'll stop believing it. Like if a shrink makes you see you believe putting your hat on the bed gives you

gonorrhea, you see that's a stupid belief and you
chuck it."

"Good luck," I said, thinking of my poor shrink
and whether he could stop my loving Noel by
showing me it was stupid.

Noel said, "I love to see swans flying together,
female and male, and you can't tell which is which. It
never occurs to him that he'd be better off if her
wings were clipped."

The Vietnam War brought out the only real
crowds. I was amazed at how everybody else was
smarter than I was about it. Somehow I'd thought
the war had nothing to do with me. It was something
the adults were doing, far away, not in my world. It
would be over before it took the boys I knew or my
brother or cousins. All they had to do to stay out of
it was go to school on and on until they were
twenty-six. Everett was about to become a Ph.D.
without ever having meant to. I didn't know anybody
too poor or too unstudious to do that.

Even when Everett and Daddy quarrelled about
the war, I didn't understand. Everett seemed to be
saying, "Stop using *my* body to act out *your*
illusions." Daddy seemed to be saying, "I fought my
war, now shut up and fight yours." I sort of dreamily
thought that was a funny thing to want for your
only son, but that was as far as I went. Daddy said,
"The war may be unjust — or just. That's not the
point. The point is, a society cannot survive if the
citizenry decides for itself which obligations to

honor," and I nodded, sound asleep, proud of his wisdom, his disinterested historical view.

Nobody else at Brundidge-Willson was that dumb. Every antiwar rally brought out hundreds, and suddenly there were speakers I'd never seen before stirring everybody up, demanding an end to war research and war recruiting on campus. They were hot and thrilling, reckless, and sometimes when the crowd was yelling, I felt something like a wave of recklessness move up my body and almost sweep my mind away. I could feel my head almost floating, almost disconnected. I almost agreed we should burn the damn country down and start over, except then there'd be nothing but broken glass and ashes and it would take forty years to make the trains run again, so maybe we should just try *fixing* the country instead — not a popular idea.

Being part of a mass instead of isolated fools was nice for a change, though, and Noel still took me home with her because we were friends by then. One night one of the hot, reckless, thrilling strangers came with us, a young woman tall and bony enough to be a model, blonde, a beauty named Wendy. I had a hard time figuring out what Wendy was talking so intensely about. It was as though I had missed the first part of a movie. Noel seemed to understand her okay, though, so I blamed myself for not knowing history, who or what was Dien Bien Phu, and so on. Dow. Napalm. Tonkin Gulf. Eisenhower's warning. Eisenhower? At last a familiar name, but what radical ever thought Eisenhower was right about anything?

"So I'm putting you in charge," Wendy said.

"Okay, but no Viet Cong flags," Noel said.

We were at Noel's place by then, and Noel was brewing up a pot of Lapsang Souchong. Wendy was sitting cross-legged on the bare floor, upright and virtuous. She scorned comfort, not that the mattress was so very comfortable either. I was lolling on it like a capitalist dog. B was sewing turquoise cloth printed with red and yellow circles.

"We honor the courage of the Liberation Front. Of course their flag will be there," Wendy said.

"That flag absolutely enrages Middle America," Noel said. "Do we want to change people's heads or don't we? Do we want to end the war or don't we?"

"Of course we do," Wendy said.

"Okay then, no flags."

Noel poured tea into mugs. B sang an inscrutable song to himself.

"But if it ends now," Wendy said slowly — embarrassed, I think, or afraid she was saying more than she should — "they won't have learned anything. When it's Latin America's turn, they'll get out the napalm again."

Noel said, "You don't want the war to end! Goddamn you, Wendy, you're trying to keep it going! You're using the flags to keep it going! You don't care about the Vietnamese or us or anything but your fucking revolution!"

"I should have known you wouldn't understand. All right, all right, no flags," Wendy said. "But you've got to force Seagirt to call the cops. Whoever calls the pigs on these bourgeois kids is *dead*."

* * * * *

The school paper ran a letter from Dr. Seagirt, the president, saying that the Brundidge-Willson campus was open to all views, including abhorrent ones, and everyone — even a war recruiter, even a napalm maker — could say what he pleased in this free place. Dr. Seagirt ended with a rousing quote from Voltaire: "I disapprove of what you say, but I will defend to the death your right to say it."

Noel was reading the letter aloud when I got to class that morning. "This is liberalism at its most glorious," she told us, "and its most contemptible. This is decadence. We'll have a protest rally this afternoon. Spread the word."

We gathered, such a horde, outside the lovely Shaker barn, chanting, "Come out! Come out!" Dr. Seagirt came out, clumsy, lumpy-haired, dressed lumpily, and climbed clumsily onto a chair. She held the wall to keep her balance. Noel — young, vigorous, sparkly, everything Dr. Seagirt was not — stood on a chair too and shouted, "We've come to discuss your letter!" through a bullhorn.

Dr. Seagirt asked, in the last of the high, quavery, Eastern-aristocratic-woman voices, "Do I get a bullhorn?" Hardly anybody could hear her. Noel could, but pretended not to. We had only one.

"You know the war is wrong," Noel intoned, "but you do not resist it. In World War Two, sixty million people died to end what the German people themselves could have ended if they had resisted what they knew was wrong."

"Hey, Seagirt! We're taking over this building!" somebody yelled. "We're gonna piss all over your office."

"Hey, Seagirt! We'll get your denture adhesive!" somebody else yelled.

"Hey, Seagirt!" Wendy yelled. I should have known she'd still be around. "We'll get your dildo!"

Over the murmur of people asking each other what's a dildo, Noel shouted, "We're going to surround the recruiting tables. We're going to intercept deliveries to the physics labs. We're going to intercept deliveries to the chemistry labs. Let's *go!* Let's *go!*" And even though Wendy was screaming, "Rush the building! Rush the building!" the crowd followed Noel, chanting, "Let's *go!* Let's *go!*" Dr. Seagirt smiled, climbed down from her chair, and limped inside. She wouldn't have to call the cops.

Wendy caught up with us. "You are shit, Noel. You are dead in the revolution. You are dead. We will not lose this historic opportunity. You'll find out what it means to be shit in the revolution. You had her head on the block, and you chickened out — because she's a goddamn dyke."

Later, when we had posted our guards and made a round-the-clock watch list, I asked Noel, "Why *did* you let her off?"

"Because she's a goddamn dyke. Of course. Solidarity. Sisterhood is powerful."

I listened, and replayed it in my head and listened again, and it was the same again. It didn't answer all my questions, such as "Then what is B to you?" but it answered yes to the question I had abandoned months before.

"I love you," I said.

"I know."

"I guess it was hard to miss."

"Yup."

We walked between banks of snow with more coming down. It was February. I had just turned nineteen.

"I used to wonder how I'd handle this when it happened," Noel said. "It was bound to happen. It's too classic not to."

"What happens?" I asked. "Classically, I mean."

"Naive student, mistaking adolescence for a tendency, mistaking admiration and loneliness for love, falls into clutches of corrupt gym teacher — English teacher — French teacher — *thing* teacher — and, A., kills herself, or, B., is rescued by a fine young man."

I said, "I like the first part."

"But times have changed. We're in a sexual revolution. A new script. A new set of rules."

"I don't know them," I said.

"They're just as harsh. *Cool* is the main rule. If you care, you can't have any."

We were at her building then. I didn't want to go up to her apartment because B would be there. He never went anywhere. But I did go into the downstairs hall with her. Somebody was playing a Beatles record very loud.

I said, "I was just kidding. I meant to say, I think you'd be fun. Kicky."

She laughed and kissed me, soft and quick. I opened my mouth for more. She closed it with her fingertip, saying, "Don't try to make anything last, even the most delicious," and kissed me again. We were exactly the same height, mouth to mouth.

She said, "I'll make you cool if I have to kiss you all night."

But instead she patted my butt and pushed me out the door.

I walked — it's fair to say, on air — back to my dormitory room. I had it to myself, always, because my roommate lived with her boyfriend off campus.

All night I stood at my window, watching the snow catch the tree branches and cling, watching the flakes slanting down in the light of the streetlamp like the bellies of a trillion silver fish, reliving Noel's kisses, thumping with rapture, praying to the god that Mother had brought home from Alcoholics Anonymous, Higher Power, often confused, Mother said, with the Japanese god Hayakawa. "H.P.," I prayed, "I need help to do this right."

Because I believed Noel absolutely. If I could keep cool, we could have great pleasure, even a sort of love. But if I got messy, it was curtains.

Next morning after class she came home with me. "This damn lobby is a mile wide," she muttered. "The whole staff is watching us cross it. They're phoning everybody they know."

She was only partly joking. I hung out my "studying" sign. I locked my door and leaned against it. I was afraid she'd never come again.

She said, "It'll be in tomorrow's paper. CHILD MOLESTER TERRORIZES STUDENT DORM."

"DISMAYED STAFF WATCHES HELPLESSLY," I intoned, luckily. The right touch. While I was hanging our snowy coats on the shower rod, she came up behind me and put her arms around me.

"You're nice and warm," she said. "That's my god, body heat. In the end, that's what heals us. Under all the brains and causes, the patient animal body making heat."

So I got a second god. "Higher Power, Body Heat, I need help to do this right," I prayed.

"I'm cold," she whined, just like Queen JoAnn, getting into my narrow bed still wearing everything except her shoes and glasses. She pulled the blankets up around her throat. Her teeth chattered fraudulently. I knew she wasn't cold.

"Me too," I said, also lying, and got in with her boldly enough, but felt shy again looking at her so close up, so different without her glasses, a whole new strange person who might not agree with Noel, who might be regretting this. Her tender brown gaze reassured me, but I felt she was waiting for me to do something wonderful, that I was being too slow, too young, too dumb, shy, and klutzy, that any minute she would hop up saying, "Thanks, don't think it hasn't been interesting," and put her glasses on. And I was also afraid of the opposite, that seeing I knew nothing she would *teach* me. "Softer, harder, higher, lower." Something like that, which is all right when your purpose is scientific, as in a game of Doctor when you're ten, but kind of off-putting in a grown-up love affair, in case that's what this turned out to be. In case I could figure out something Noel liked enough to come back for more of. I was going to have to figure out something soon. Kissing her was heavenly enough for me, but how long would a woman of the world lie still for just that?

My only experience was Doctor and King Albert–Queen JoAnn, about as worldly as giggling

over dirty words, but what to do? I put my mouth
the scientific distance from Noel's ear, not so close as
to boom but close enough for breath to be warm, and
whispered, "You're so beautiful. Your eyes are so
soft."

She faked a pretty good amused cool, whispering,
"That is called myopia," but I felt the shiver in her.
I knew I had her, and felt confidence fill me like gas
filling a balloon. That's not called inflation for
nothing. I moved on to neck-nape, reached under her
sweater for nipples, and all the great places on back
and side that vibrate when delicately scratched with
the corner of a fingernail, and when she trembled and
gasped, "Oh, Patricia, you are divine!" I knew how
men felt, like I really could go out and earn the
bread. I felt like the winner and new champion,
entitled to sole possession of Noel, not by brute force,
law, or custom, by no power but delight. I came very
near to commanding, "Don't let B do this!"

Thanks to Higher Power, though, I kept my
mouth shut, so we still had several exciting times
together. But the idea of Noel's being with a man
bothered me more and more. When I finally risked
uttering my command, several weeks later, it was no
longer power I wanted, but less discomfort, fewer
dismaying images.

"Don't let B do this?" I whimpered, not
commandingly

Noel got up and put her glasses on.

Getting dressed, she said, "Tonight in New York
City at eight o'clock sharp, one million dykes will
chant in unison, 'Bisexuality is the ideal. Why cut out
half the human race?' But try *being* bisexual, baby,
and see where it gets you. It gets you nothing but

men, is what it gets you. And all those kindly,
liberated, unjudging dykes will run away from you in
droves and platoons and *armies.*"

I sat on the edge of my bed watching for the last
time as her dear body disappeared into clothes. "I
haven't run away," I said. "It's just —"

"That I seem vaguely contaminated, right? Don't
think I haven't noticed your — omissions."

"Well, uh, if you could —"

"Forget it. This was always a bad idea."

I was afraid I'd have a hard time, that class might
be painful, and so on. But because I'd always known
Noel and I had no future, I didn't feel so bad.
There's a minute or two at the beginning of these
things, I think, when you can still choose how much
of your gut to risk.

If Noel had ever said she loved me, I might have
revised my first estimate and got in too far.

I thank her for being careful of me.

But I was awake again, tired of being cool, tired
of not daring to care or ask for what I needed, and
two doors down the hall lived Marina, who was
forever joining me at dinner, shyly, or leaving shy
notes that said drop by later if you feel like it. She
even came to some demonstrations, but never got so
she could shout.

A suitor, I thought. This time I'll be the one who
makes the rules, I thought. And if Marina gets soppy
and messy, I thought, so much the better. After Noel,
soppy would look good.

I began dropping by. Under Marina's commonplace prettiness, some beauty could be detected, something possibly genuine and human, something able to do heroic things quietly. A real woman! A Pilgrim Mother who wouldn't mind that the Pilgrim song would leave her out, that it would be about me!

She felt so silly prattling about her silly life, she said. Or she felt so guilty heaping all her problems on me instead of being funny and fun.

Her problem was that her parents were divorcing. They said they'd been wanting to for years and only waiting for her to grow up. "But I'm *not* grown up. Why can't they see?"

I listened on and on. "Nothing in the world feels safe anymore!" she'd cry. There was a lot of repetition. "I'm losing my home!" she'd cry. Other people's problems are so much easier to bear than one's own. I'd just notice how nice her mouth looked and wonder if I dared kiss it, and wonder why I didn't dare. What was Marina doing, after all, but begging me to dare — so something could happen that wouldn't be her fault, that just happened?

She'd say she wished she could be more like me, good-looking and together and smart and confident and sane. Everything she said seemed simply true, not at all excessive. She said just being near me made her feel amazingly good, she didn't know why. Made her feel grown-up after all, maybe, but (joke) she wouldn't want her parents to know that and feel free about divorcing. A daughter more like me and less like herself might have made her parents happy and proud enough to stay together.

How much praise and reassurance did I need? I didn't touch Marina even when she wept, when any humane person would have. I too was waiting for something to happen by itself and not be my fault.

Toward Christmas, Marina came stumbling into my room. I was sitting at my desk. She was blind with tears, bumping into things. It was happening by itself! I had no choice but to hold her on my lap. She had no choice but to press against me, because through no fault of ours her parents had phoned in quick succession to tell her to choose between them at Christmas time. "He said *he's* expecting me. She said *she's* expecting me. What am I supposed to do? Why are they driving me crazy? She'll never forgive me if I go to him. He'll never forgive me if I go to her. It's so unfair. Why do they want to drive me crazy?"

I kissed Marina's tears away, saying, "Come home with me."

"Oh, I couldn't! It would kill them. Do you think I could? It would serve them right."

Her eyes and cheeks were all nicely mopped up, but I kept on kissing them. "You'll like my house." Kiss. "You'll like my family." Kiss.

"I will," Marina said. "I'll do it. They can go to hell."

"Right," I said, and kissed her lips.

"Patricia, don't."

"I didn't know this was going to happen," I said, kissing her again.

"Oh, what have I done?"

"Nothing. It's just happening. By itself."

"No, no, I let you get the wrong impression."

When did she get so smart? She had never been smart before.

"I didn't mean to," she said. "I like you, but I don't love you. I mean, I love you, but not like that."

"Okay. Please get off my leg. It's gone to sleep."

She stood up. "You're mad at me," she said.

"No I'm not."

"You don't want me to come for Christmas now."

"Sure I do. Go away and let me tell Mother." I tore a sheet out of my notebook and clicked my ballpoint pen.

Marina turned at the door, saying, "It's nothing against you."

"I know," I said, writing nonsense syllables seriously.

"I'm just a very conventional person, I guess."

"I know."

"If it could be a girl, it would be you."

"I know."

"I don't care if you're like that."

The only thing I'm not ashamed of in all this is that I did not say, "I'm *not* like that."

She asked, "Can we still be friends?"

"Yup."

"You can be your way and I can be my way and we can be friends anyway, right?"

"Will you please go away and let me write to Mother?"

"I'm afraid things will be different."

"No they won't. Just go," I said, and at last she did.

Then came my tears, not a flood, but several. I was surprised at any. It wasn't that I had let myself

get hooked or anything. And there was nothing to
worry about. Once Marina got used to the idea,
wouldn't she have to come through for me? What
with loving me and all?

One of my least favorite things about Everett was
that he called me "Sis" and chuckled fraternally
when other people were around, after ignoring me all
the rest of the time. He did it again when I took
Marina home. You'd have thought we were a loving
family. He even hugged me, but I felt him looking
across my head to Marina.

I don't mean he shouldn't have loved her. He
should have loved her later, after he'd seen more in
her than prettiness, that's all.

She loved him right away too. I thought it was
because they'd be a handsome couple. He was looking
good: modified hippie, red hair half long, jeans half
shabby, and a sort of solid air about him as his Ph.D.
came closer, ready to state important opinions slowly.
I didn't find out until years later how commonplace it
is to love a dyke and marry her brother or husband
— whichever male stands closest to her.

It's not up to me to celebrate the dreary little ups
and downs of Everett and Marina. It's their world. I
am here for my own people.

School was a lousy place for love affairs. I
couldn't control my environment or my society. Year
after year I had to keep on seeing the one who didn't

take me seriously and the one who liked my brother better than me. I couldn't get a new address and a whole new set of people.

However, school was a good place for study, once I switched to psychology. Majoring in art had come close to withering my hand. Psychology was my hiding place while the painter in me healed up and started to grow. No teacher would ever interfere with my painter again.

CHAPTER TWO:
Sharon

I lived in a beat-up old tenement on East Ninth
Street, sixth floor. There were sunny windows for
plants, and a fireplace I brought broken-up crates and
wood scraps to. Otherwise the place wasn't much,
your basic slum, and really bare except for a mattress
on the floor with pretty sheets and blankets I bought.
I couldn't afford new furniture and didn't want old
— because I was born under Leo, Grandma says —
but bare or not, the place was my home and I loved

it. I used to leap up those five flights of stairs two steps at a time and shut my door behind me and lean back and feel the walls sort of hug me, because they were mine.

I saw quite a lot of the Mothers. They invited me to come along on their Sunday walks. They were exploring the city a neighborhood at a time and taking pictures.

The first time, before I knew better, I showed up on Perry Street wearing my regular pants and boots.

Mother Two said, "Didn't you know we were going to Rockefeller Center?"

"I may not have told her," Mother One lied. She was always trying to undo Mother Two's toughness, not knowing I sort of liked it.

Mother Two gave me a stern look, saying, "We never go above Fourteenth Street in pants, Kiddo," like she thought I'd bring the vice squad down on us. She was dressed in an old familiar nylon jersey dress and looked a lot butchier in it than she ever would in pants. She looked like a little padded truck. Big soft Mother One towered over her but still seemed to smell of cookie dough and baby powder.

M-2 decided against Rockefeller Center. We went down to the Wall Street district, which is safely deserted on Sundays. I'd been down there a lot already, professionally, and figured I could impress the Mothers with what I knew, but they were only interested in whatever little sooty leftover from olden times they could find among the wonderful new glassy towers that looked like light and air held up by magic. Crumbling red brick was what the Mothers were after, and tombstones in churchyards, that you don't have to be in New York to see. What I liked best of what we saw that day was a huge mass of sunflowers blossoming block after block in the rubble where land had been cleared for the World Trade Center. Mother One said, "It shows nature will heal herself no matter what we do."

"It shows somebody had a lot of sunflower seeds," Mother Two grumped, to seem sensible, but she snapped a dozen pictures.

I said, "I promise I'll wear a skirt if you'll ask me again."

"See that you do," Mother Two said.

We went out winter and summer, all weathers. Sometimes the camera shutter froze. Sometimes our clothes stuck to us with sweat. We saw things I'd have missed or not noticed without the Mothers, like Tiffany windows in a church in Brooklyn, and pigeons keeping warm on electric signs, and Susan B. Anthony in the Hall of Fame in the Bronx. Women must always vote, for her sake, M-1 said.

We saw buildings made of iron you could stick a magnet to, and gods and lions carved on windowframes. At the Cloisters we saw a statue that looked like Mary being tired and proud of Baby Jesus, but it was St. Anne lying with newborn Baby Mary, it was a *girl!* We went to Poe Cottage. We took the ferry to Staten Island and then a bus to a Tibetan museum full of weird statues the Mothers liked but I didn't. They liked the incense there too. We saw a man standing on the back end of the ferryboat singing "America the Beautiful" to the Statue of Liberty, and not caring if he was a fool. Of course he was, but we didn't care either.

Always we carried a guidebook, map, and camera, and everybody kept asking, "Are you lost? Can I help you?" And I mean, in Harlem too, where everybody said don't go, they'll mug you.

Once when we were sitting on a pier watching the tide make the Hudson run backward, M-1 invited me to a party.

M-2 looked so unpleased I was afraid she'd un-invite me, but all she said was, "You'll be meeting important people, professional people. I trust you know how to keep your mouth shut."

"Of course she does," M-1 said.

"We don't know that."

"Well, we know her father didn't come after us with a gun. We know we didn't lose our jobs."

Until then I hadn't known what the fuss was about. Of course if people could lose their jobs or something, it was right to be careful. But how did they ever find each other or make friends if everybody was careful?

I said, "I didn't tell."

"Then that's settled," M-1 said.

"Lucille, sometimes you're so naive."

I said, "Look, if it makes you uptight, I don't have to."

"No, it's okay," M-2 said.

I almost didn't go. How could I have a good time if everybody was afraid I'd blackmail them? But I was lonely, and these were the people I had come to New York to find, so I went.

To please Mother Two, I wore a dress and sandals. I combed my lion's mane straight out into a sort of WASP Afro. It looked a little longer, but not more respectable. I still felt like a street kid from the slums.

There were ten or twelve women at the party when I got there, all, to tell the truth, awfully old, and more kept arriving in pairs, old too. From how disappointed I felt, I saw I'd been hoping to find somebody. Why else would I care how ancient they were?

They seemed to like each other, though, and kept smiling and greeting each other with hugs and little lip kisses and dancing together to old music that just oozed along without a real beat.

They weren't interested in me at all. I mostly sat by myself on the woodbox, petting Mother One's big gray cat, which spurted hairs at every touch, and watching. That funny old dancing turned out to be really sexy. How their bodies touched from top to bottom. How like in a dream they drifted together. How gently they moved. How beautiful they got. I liked their clothes — faded knee-length shorts, soft shirts. Nobody but me wore a dress. I never would again. I wanted to be like them, wanted to belong with them, wanted to figure out their ways and copy them.

Mother One stopped dancing and sat down beside me. She said, "You're looking very pretty. I hope you're enjoying yourself at some level."

"I am," I said.

"I should have warned you, lesbians are not friendly folk. We tend not to talk to anybody we don't know. I've never met one who knows how to circulate at a party. We have no small talk. Mustn't, of course, say, 'Whereabouts you from?' or 'What do you do for a living?' So it all takes a while. Don't take it personally. Don't get discouraged. In due time, we're quite nice."

"I'm in love with everybody here," I said.

"That's a relief. I myself was very excited when Vera and I first made some friends. I was wild, in fact. Free at last! Home at last! All that."

"Yeah," I said. "Me too."

"I'll be glad when enthusiasm comes back in style. You looked so self-possessed I couldn't tell. Here you sat, cross-legged, perfectly contained. Poised. Thinking us over. A little judgmental, maybe. But all the while there's this lunatic in you? Really? Wild with joy?"

"Yeah," I said, trying to stay cool but smiling my big uncool smile. Other people can smile reasonable smiles, but with me it's got to be ear-to-ear or nothing.

"Come with me," she said, leading me to the kitchen. "There's someone I want you to meet."

I hoped it would be someone to love, but someone to like was almost as good, and she was also someone to work for and learn from, Marnie Fellowes, who ran a combination health bar and herb shop on West Eleventh Street.

Marnie was beside the refrigerator waving her arms and yelling about something the Food and Drug Administration had done, and she wasn't easy to get the attention of, but Mother One kept at her.

"Marnie, this is the kid whose letter I showed you, Sharon."

"Is she okay?"

"She's more than okay."

Marnie looked at me. I still hadn't come down from my huge smile. She gave me one too, but smaller, and said, "I like your looks. You look healthy. You look happy. Those are the vibes I want in my herbs. But I don't know. Oh, what the hell. Let's give it a try. Want to?"

I was getting tired of messenger work, all the beautiful people who didn't give a big rat's ass what a kindred soul I was. It would feel pretty good to stay in one place and get to know somebody, starting with Marnie. I liked her looks, too. Middle-sized, brown hair going gray, but best I liked how she wasn't uptight, how easy her smile was, how she got worked up and waved her arms. Her spirit, I mean.

I didn't ask any of the sensible questions about pay and hours and duties. I just said, "Sure," and smiled again.

I liked working at The Rose Hip. I could wear my same comfortable clothes, except I had to be more sure they were freshly washed, and I had to shampoo my hair more often — hard because I had no shower, just a claw-foot tub in my kitchen. Marnie wanted me to sort of glow, to suggest if you bought her stuff you would too.

The store was nice, especially the first few breaths in the morning before my nose got used to it and stopped registering. There were shelves from floor to ceiling filled with jars of dried herbs and bottles of tinctures and decoctions and lotions, jars of ointment. There was a little library so people could look up their symptoms and ask for the remedy, because it was against the law for Marnie to prescribe, but she did it anyway if you kept coming back enough and she figured you weren't a cop. At the back was a counter where we sold really good food, thick soup, carrot or minty cucumber juice, and wonderful sandwiches — like mashed avocado, goat cheese, and sprouts on brown bread we made ourselves in plain view, no partition. Lots of our customers were first brought in by the smell of baking bread blowing out to the sidewalk.

Marnie gave me the dumb jobs, like scrubbing organic loam off of carrots and dusting the herb jars and rinsing the sprouts. We sprouted radish seeds, things you didn't see everywhere then. Flax, sesame, dill, fenugreek, peanuts, chick peas, along with common alfalfa and mung beans.

Marnie worked the counter because that was where people talked about their troubles, like they never did just browsing the shelves. They'd sit there eating and pretty soon she'd know all about their insomnia and their bowels, their cold, their lame knee, their headache, the cramp in their leg. Then Marnie would send me up the ladder for a jar of something — sweet woodruff, comfrey, burdock root, dandelion, marsh mallow, uva ursi, devil's claw — which she measured out on an old-timey balance scale with pans and weights. She'd actually ask people, while they were *eating*, what color their shit was and if it floated. That took some getting used to, for me, but it never bothered them. I guess everybody's interested in their own shit.

One day when there weren't any customers, I sat down at the counter. I ordered a glass of minty cucumber juice and sipped it sadly, like a troubled customer. "I'm a lesbian and I have no lover," I said. "Do you have a specific for that?"

"Not in stock," Marnie said, looking at me as carefully as she did at any other sufferer. "Have you ever had a lover?"

"Sort of. We didn't call it that."

"So you don't really know what you are or what you want."

She never asked people if they were sure their knees really hurt.

"I do, though," I said, turning away because I saw I was going to get a lecture and no help or even sympathy. I would have settled for sympathy.

"You had a little schoolgirl thing, and you're going to let that govern your whole life?" she yelled, waving her arms. I was sorry I'd ever liked how she got excited and waved her arms. That was when she wasn't doing it at me. "You should be in college. You should be dating boys. Give them a chance, Sharon. What do *you* know?"

If some girl said she liked boys, would Marnie say, hey, kid, give girls a chance?

To tell the truth, I despised Marnie a little. I knew she didn't even mean any of that, except maybe college. She was just playing it safe, so nobody could blame her for anything later on. Me right there with an aching heart should have been more important to her than what some possible stranger might say someday.

I took up my featherduster and flicked away at the herb jars, to show her the consultation was over and she could shut up. But she kept on, raising her voice to make me listen, but I fooled her and didn't. Something about the world's many marvelous possibilities and so on. Rave on, Marnie. How I shouldn't close any doors so young, and so on. How if I wanted a lover, I had to *look* for one.

What?

I went back to my glass of cucumber juice.

"Did you ever hear of A.P.F.U.? Also called Ap-Foo?" she asked. "A Place for Us? They're in the phone book. Give them a call. Find out when they meet."

They met on Thursday evenings in an upstairs room on West Thirty-First Street. For many a Thursday I hid in the shadows and watched the women go in, but couldn't get up the nerve to go in myself. They weren't like the women at the party. Some of them looked tough. I suspect Mother Two was tougher than any of them, but she didn't *look* it. Some of them looked like pairs of men and women, slicked-back short hair on one, upswept beehive hair and makeup on the other.

I began to wonder if Marnie had sent me there to see I didn't want that life after all.

But there were ordinary women, too, some my age even, or just about, and I got tired of being a coward and went up the stairs. What could happen?

I found a folding chair at the very back of the room and did my best to disappear in it. They were having a group discussion, Butch and Femme: Myth or Reality? They were supposed to say myth, but a lot said, "As for me it is reality." Just as I was getting interested, someone who said she was president came over and asked me how old I was.

"Twenty."

"Sorry. You have to be twenty-one."

"I meant, twenty-one."

She laughed. "Come back in a year," she said. "Sorry."

So I had to leave, but someone followed and caught up with me at the bottom of the stairs, really neat-looking. "I couldn't help noticing you," she said.

It helped that she was dressed in jeans and boots like me. Otherwise she would have been just too much. Blonde, great build, pure clean happy face. Marnie would have hired her.

We went to a coffee shop and talked a while. She said, "I'm the Huckleberry Muffin Queen, but you can call me Candi, with an i." She said Ap-Foo was a drag, a timid bunch, no fun, except when somebody like me showed up. Which didn't happen often, she said, and when they did, wouldn't you know they'd get kicked out?

"Which are you, butch or femme," she asked.

I didn't know, so I stalled by saying, "Isn't that a myth?"

"No. So which are you?"

"Which are you?" I asked.

"I'm butch."

"I'm femme," I said.

"Want to come to my place?" she asked.

"All right," I said, scared of nothing except not knowing how to do whatever she was expecting.

On the bus, she pushed her thigh against mine. I wouldn't have believed I could get that turned on by somebody I didn't love and maybe didn't even like, on a bus. She stared straight ahead and popped her chewing gum. The cinnamon smell of it, her little mouth sounds, the heat of her thigh flowing into my thigh and on up.

She was expecting nothing except reaction, and I gave her plenty of it up there in her loft bed with her cats all over us. When I tried to roll her over and do something back, she wouldn't let me. "Butches are givers. I'm satisfied," she said, and she sure did look it. She looked, in fact, very conceited. I suspected her of thinking butches were better than femmes, but I'd fight that out another time. Right then everything just felt so good.

We were at it all night, with little rests, and in the morning when I was putting my crunchy underpants back on to go to work, not tired, she said, "Come back tonight?"

"All right."

Marnie took one look at me and said, "Feel better?"

"Yeah. It's funny. I don't even love her."

"There's something to be said for lust, too. It's as rare as love, actually."

"What do you know about butches?"

Marnie laughed.

I said, "Really. Tell me."

"Well, they're a curious race. Somebody said they're an adolescent girl's imitation of Humphrey Bogart."

"She wouldn't let me — uh —"

"Some of them let you. They know they're going out of style, and they want to keep up with the times. So they lie there like a board. They spread their legs one inch. And it's your fault — you're an ignorant blunderer. They met you halfway, didn't they? They didn't freak out, did they? What more do you want?"

She laughed tenderly. I could see she had a lot of happy memories.

She said, "They think they want to feel as much as you feel. They think if you were an expert lover, like *them*, they would. They envy you. You've got *them*, and all they've got is *you*.. No fair! And the next thing you know, the last thing you'd ever expect, they're crawling around after some damn butch. It lasts from before Thanksgiving until after New Year's — just long enough to wreck your holidays. They come back in January. Does that answer your question?"

I sure liked how Marnie opened up at last and talked to me, but I knew better than to believe everything she said. I knew, no matter how many lovers she'd had, she couldn't know about *every*body.

I guess butches were her favorite topic. She couldn't stop. I was up on the ladder dusting, and she was looking up, chattering away. I loved it.

"If you're lucky, they come back a little wiser," she said. "They know how much courage it takes to be vulnerable. They know they're not your boss. They know sexual surrender is not surrender at all."

I didn't want to look too deep and spoil how simply good Candi made my body feel. Friday and Saturday nights it felt even better. She did some extras, like dragging her hair along my back, and

wetting my neck with her tongue and blowing on it.
She was welcome to think she had me in her power.
I was in no shape to argue the point. If she roared in
triumph when her fingers came into me, what did I
care? We both yelled our heads off and the neighbors
pounded the walls, shouting, "Shut up in there!" and
I still didn't care.

But I did not love her.

Sunday morning we had to go out for cat food.
The cats, Abyssinian royalty it turned out, would eat
nothing but a certain brand of canned chicken breast,
which the corner store was out of. We had to go
down Third Avenue to a deli.

A man in a fancy convertible pulled alongside us,
saying, "Hi, girls."

We ignored him and walked on, past all the
closed-up Sunday-morning stores. He crept his car
along the curb saying stuff like, "Don't be that way.
You're both so pretty, and I'm man enough for both
of you."

"Not interested, Mister," I said.

"Oh, so it's that way! Hey, you're making a big
mistake!"

"Leave us alone, Mister," Candi said.

"Come on! Come on! I can show you a really good
time," he said.

Candi walked over and stood beside his car. She
looked very beautiful. He got all excited. She was
wearing her big yellow stomping boots, and she
hauled off and gave his car a kick you could hear for
three blocks.

"Hey, mister, y'got a dent in your car!" she said.

He hit his gas pedal so hard his tires left marks.

I almost loved Candi then.

But not quite. She had bad habits. For instance, sometimes she'd look at me fondly and say, "Penny." Naturally, I'd politely pretend I didn't know what she meant, and she'd have to say, "Penny for your *thoughts*," disgusted at how stupid I was. But I never told her my thoughts. Sexual surrender is not surrender.

Other times she'd look at me fondly and say, "Y.T.M.O.," which she had to explain meant You Turn Me On. It reminded me of a Catholic church back home named Church of the B.V.M. Some people will abbreviate anything.

"How A that?" I'd say.

Candi didn't love me, either. At least I hope not. I know she very much wanted me to love her, but that's not the same thing. I don't think I hurt her, and she did me a lot of good at just the right time. Remembering her always makes me feel good.

CHAPTER THREE:
Patricia

My train came in at Grand Central. I took a cab to Sharon's building. Her mother had given me the address. She was remorseful enough to give me anything. I wish I'd known that sooner.

The cab driver said, "I advise you not to get out, Miss. This is a dangerous neighborhood." I paid him and got out. He lingered worriedly. I climbed Sharon's stoop and rang her bell, a savvy urbane world traveler, and waved him away.

In the bright daylight nothing looked so bad, merely dirty, merely shabby, but Sharon didn't answer and I had to wait. And wait. And wait. I sat on a milk crate across the street to watch for her. Evening came. Well-dressed people carrying groceries came home from work. Transformed into hippies, they came out again led by dogs. They came out again at nine to buy the next day's *Times*. Still no Sharon. Darkness came. The stoop of her building filled up with sleeping drunks and junkies. Street musicians played Dixieland scarily well. Was this how America cared for its artists? Was this how it would care for me? Prostitutes climbed into slowly cruising cars. Midnight came. Stray cats and dogs unhid. Rats examined the garbage and stared at me. What was I doing on their turf? I had to agree.

I went over to the avenue, held up my hand for a cab, and went to the Abbey Victoria, a tacky hotel I'd stayed in with my family once when we came to see Daddy get a prize.

The desk clerk wasn't sure he should let me in. Alone, I was undesirable. No reservation? Just this backpack? Cash? Didn't I have a credit card? Well! He was just enjoying his little power, spinning it out, making it last.

If Sharon was dead, I'd forgive her. If, as I suspected, she was sleeping with someone else, watch out!

I collapsed into the musty bed the clerk finally granted me, and though hungry, fell asleep at once.

I dreamed that Earth had been captured by space people, who penned us up in little groups while they tried to decide whether to kill us. My group was in the great hall of Grand Central, the one with the zodiac and stars on the ceiling. Sharon's group was herded in. When she saw me, she risked being killed to break away from her guards and run to me and kiss and hold me. We both sobbed with joy at seeing each other one more time before we died. The space people watched us. They consulted among themselves. They sent for their leader, whose sex I could not determine. She/He declared the whole world free, because Sharon and I had demonstrated that Earthlings have the capacity to rise above simple animal reflexes. So we saved humanity with our love, as Jung suspected we might.

That was one of the great clear dreams of my life. It made the frustrations of yesterday fade away, just not matter. What did I expect when I hadn't let Sharon know I was coming?

In the morning I phoned Mrs. Almo, who told me where Sharon worked. The Rose Hip. It was in the phone book. West Eleventh Street.

The Rose Hip's door was locked against robbers. I had to rap on the glass and be looked at before the gray-haired owner buzzed me in. I pushed open the door and was hit, as by heat from an oven, with a blast of fragrance, a mingling of all the innocent, earthy plants of paradise like raspberry and willow and clover and geranium, mixed with baking bread. It was simply beautiful. It made me want to be a better person, more wholesome and plain.

When I went in, a lovely whiff went out and converted some other people to clean living too. They too discovered that across the sidewalk from the fuming trucks was a little capsule of primeval air, something divine.

So the shop was busy, right when I was hoping

Sharon could get the day off. She was up on a ladder flicking at jars with a featherduster. She didn't notice me, so I had a chance to look at her.

Our six years apart hadn't changed her much. She was still my fresh, rosy, lovely Queen JoAnn, perhaps somewhat taller, her bones perhaps better defined, elegant at the wrist.

"Where have you been?" I asked.

She looked down at me. She grabbed her ladder, not to fall. She stayed that way, stuck, but smiling her glorious all-out smile and looking down at me. I had a flash of déjà vu while my face was tipped up to her smile, but it passed and I said again, "Where have you been?"

"Where have *you* been?" she asked.

"On East Ninth Street, looking for you."

Her smile stopped. "I guess I wasn't home," she said, all flustered.

"No," I said.

"What are you doing here? I mean, what's the backpack? Are you on your way somewhere, or what?"

"That depends.

"Where are you staying?"

"That depends."

Her boss said, "Sorry, Sharon, you mustn't talk with your hands empty," and gestured toward a bushel of dirty carrots.

Sharon climbed down, saying, "Marnie, this is Patricia Burley. We go way back."

"It shows," Marnie said. "I hate to dampen a sweet reunion, but please keep breathing."

I said, "I can come back later."

"No, no," Marnie said. She took hold of my arm

and backed me around the end of the counter. "If you stand right here, you won't be underfoot."

So I stood there at the sink beside Sharon while her nice hands washed carrots. Marnie was rapidly turning them into juice for her little crowd of customers.

"So tell me everything," Sharon said.

"I came to be a painter and to find you," I said.

There was a pause in the sink. Then Sharon said, slowly, "Your folks won't like that."

"Maybe not. They want me to go to graduate school. They say a bachelor's degree in psychology is worthless. They're right, of course."

"They'll have a fit," Sharon said.

I hadn't come all this way and sat among the rats at midnight to listen to the same garbage I could hear inside my own head, so I ignored her.

I said, "Majoring in art almost wrecked me. I worried was it good design? Was it derivative? Was it facile? Was it cutesy? I was so damn uptight. I was critical before I could get anything on the paper to be critical *of*. But I saved myself. I had to start over, with princesses. I got myself back. I'm okay."

Sharon said, "Your folks will have a fit."

"Are you living with anybody?" I asked.

"No." *That* was what I had sat among the rats to hear.

"Got room for me?"

"Sure. But it's not much of a place. And your folks will have a fit."

"You could sound a little happy."

"I am. But your folks will have a fit."

She would require wooing. I didn't worry. I was experienced.

"I'll get your dinner," I said.

She gave me her keys. I left my backpack for her to bring home and went up to Grand Central after the big seabag I'd left in the checkroom. I remembered the bag as really heavy, but somehow it felt so light that day.

Everything that day was light, easy, and beautiful. The people on the subway were beautiful. Where else could I give a stranger's face more than a glance? Of course I had to pretend I wasn't looking. Pretend I was woolgathering, half asleep, unfocussed. Look slightly to one side.

The spray-painted graffiti were beautiful, so brilliant and dense, web on web. A determined citizenry had come forward and against all opposition turned the subway system into an endless gallery of Jackson Pollocks.

I bought beautiful brown eggs and green onions and a green pepper and some cheese and butter from a little store in our neighborhood to make omelets, and grapes and shasta daisies from open stalls, explaining that I was moving in with Sharon and loving New York. How can people buy things without saying anything to the clerk? Not quite as light, I climbed the long stairs. I admit I was panting by the time I unlocked the door and looked around at Sharon's empty, comfortless barracks.

"Oh, Sharon, you've really needed me," I whispered, gasping but undismayed. Eager, in fact, to get started. Noel and Bassikounou had made a cozy home out of less than this, and my mother on a larger scale had too. Nest building was in my blood. I could hardly wait. Shaker-white walls brightened by my paintings. Furniture judiciously selected from the streets, other people's castoffs. I would refinish and repair it. The good smells of cooking. A fire on the grate. Our little home.

When I plugged in my tiny plastic radio, lovely Clementi poured out, as clear and big as on Daddy's fancy sound system. Bless New York for its fine stations. Bless WBAI, WNYC, WNCN, WQXR.

Apparently Sharon didn't eat at home much. Her one frying pan was dusty from disuse. I washed it and cut up the omelet stuff. Then I started a picture on the brown grocery bag with felt-tipped pens, all colors. A red-haired princess with crown and train. Better make that two princesses.

"Five o'clock and sunny in New York," the radio said. "And now the news. Police, fearing a recurrence of last night's homosexual rioting, are deploying tactical forces around Sheridan Square."

My hand stopped. My breath stopped. "Damn!" I said.

"An early-morning police raid on the Stonewall Inn, a Christopher Street after-hours bar frequented by homosexuals, encountered jeers and a hail of coins. Full-scale rioting developed in nearby Sheridan Square when police transferred arrested patrons to vans. Rioters broke windows and set trash fires. Police expressed surprise. 'Usually they just run away or beg us or try to bribe us to let them go. There's never been anything like this,' said one officer."

I was too upset to finish my picture. Why did this bunch of nutty ruffians have to go wild and get us into the news right when I was starting my home with Sharon and wanted nothing but obscurity and peace?

I pushed up the dirty window and leaned out. My

elbows got all gritty. The view of the street was much like the one from the sixth balcony at the opera. I saw dwarfed, foreshortened figures in bus-size clumps. One of them at last was Sharon, striding along with my backpack and a fistful of daisies. She didn't look up. I hoped she didn't know about the rioting. If she knew, wouldn't she have told me about it at the Rose Hip? I started the omelet.

She was up the stairs sooner than possible, holding out the daisies. She said, "Hi. We have to go to Sheridan Square." She went to a cross on the wall and turned it so "to dare" was on top.

"Not me," I said, putting her daisies into the peanut butter jar with mine. I don't think she noticed mine.

"You don't understand," she said. "We have to. It's a demonstration for gay rights."

"They're not demonstrating, they're rioting. And the cops are waiting to club them, and they'll get brain damage, and for what?"

"For me," Sharon said.

"For nothing. For nobody. To make a noise. Get washed. Supper's almost ready."

I had pictured us sitting crosslegged on the mattress and smiling at each other while we ate. Instead we walked around with our plates and kept on fighting. One omelet was enough and we left most of it.

On and on we wrangled, storming and repeating. I was trying to make our fight last until it was too late to go to the riot, but I knew I couldn't. I knew the riot had more energy than we did.

At last Sharon said, "You're just like Marnie! How'd you get to be old like Marnie? All afternoon I begged her to come with us tonight. She kept saying it's their problem, the guys'. *We* don't get in trouble. Nobody bothers *us*. *We* don't grope strangers in public toilets."

I said, "I'm not saying that. We do get in trouble. My father's giving me hell. I can't go to the Old Place because he thinks I'm a menace to the children. He won't sign a paper I need to get some money my grandmother left me, because he says I'm not a well person. All I'm saying is that throwing bottles and setting fires isn't going to make my father change his mind. All right?"

"I have to go, if you do or don't," Sharon said.

"Did you hear anything I said?"

"Yes. But I have to go anyway. Please come too."

"No."

She headed for the door. With her hand on the knob she turned and said, "I'm scared. If I disappeared, nobody'd know it. Please come too."

"No!" I said it tougher than I felt. I hoped she couldn't see that I'd have go to with her if she went.

"I hate being a coward," she whispered.

"You're not a coward, and I'm not either."

"Yes you are, and now I am too."

"Listen, Sharon!" I yelled. "I've marched and demonstrated against the Vietnam War and for abortion and black civil rights and God knows what all, when sometimes it was nobody but me and my friend Noel marching, and if you think a coward could do that —"

"You marched for everybody but us," Sharon said.

"When there's an orderly demonstration, I'll go. I promise," I said. "But I will not riot." I was trying to give her a way out, a way to give up.

She laid herself face-down on the mattress. I knelt beside her and took her hand. "This isn't the reunion I had in mind," I said.

"I'm ashamed," she said, rolling to face away from me but leaving her hand in mine. "I should be there. I shouldn't be letting other people fight my fight."

I leaned across her back and kissed her temple. The fragrance of the Rose Hip was in her hair.

She said, "I don't believe you'll ever go to a demonstration."

"Wait and see," I murmured, kissing her cheek. I poured love, but there was nothing coming back from her except a sort of rigid grief. I didn't care. At least her head wasn't broken.

I stayed beside her because the mattress was the only furniture. In time, not touching, we fell asleep.

The damn riots went on for two more nights, and Sharon was mad at me the whole time. She was free to stop at Sheridan Square after work and wait around for the action to begin, and there wouldn't have been a thing I could do to stop her. But she didn't seem to realize that, and I didn't tell her.

She never did get over blaming me for our not assisting at the birth of the revolution that began when a drag queen hit a cop with his purse.

I wondered why she blamed me. Why not whoever she had been with that night I spent among the rats? Why not Marnie? Why not her precious Mothers One and Two?

But I knew why. It was because I was the most

important. So I couldn't feel very insulted. I felt, in fact, very serene and energetic, and began at once to make our home.

Three coats of white paint and a whole day's work transformed the front room. It became bright, simple and pure. Sharon seemed not impressed. We went on with our fight.

I said, "Can we change the subject? Can we have a *lovers'* quarrel? You know I love you. What's the matter?"

"I don't know," she said sadly. "I think maybe I kept my hands behind my back so long, about you, they froze there."

Once more we fell asleep without touching.

If she hadn't unhesitatingly let me live with her and be highhanded with her walls, and if she hadn't come right home every evening instead of going wherever she had gone before, I might have had to wonder if she still loved me.

I was determined to paint a lot of pictures and sell them on the street for whatever people would pay, however little, and live on it. My hero was Grandma Moses, who started painting when her eyes got too dim for needlework, and took her first picture to the store like any other farm product, like eggs or butter. After she died her family collected some of her things in an old one-room schoolhouse, to celebrate her long, busy, no-nonsense life, and to make some money, I suppose. They charged admission. She wouldn't have minded that. Her mixing bowl was there, her kneading board, and, best, the old kitchen table where she painted, the mayonnaise jar lids she mixed her paints in. Mother and I went there once without Daddy. Grandma Moses wasn't his kind of history. I stood there a long time trying to open my pores and take in her vibes. Trying to be possessed by her and become innocent and practical like her. While staying entirely myself, of course.

Maybe I didn't want Grandma Moses's difficult heterosexual life, but I wanted to be a genius and have a table to be a genius at, and a chair, please, too. Somebody would throw out the perfect table and chair. It happened all the time, and I'd be waiting. Noel had told me there were people in New York who looked on the streets for exactly what they needed, such as a teak board ten feet and one inch long, or three yards of purple polka-dot linen, or a chandelier, and they always found it, but not immediately.

Since I still had a little money, I could wait for my table and take a few days to explore the great art museums. I liked the madonnas at the Metropolitan, once I realized that the artists had painted in little jokes, to protest having to please the church. Sometimes it took me a while to find the joke, but it was always there. Like maybe Baby Jesus is retarded, or maybe Mary's dropping him, or she's nauseated at the sight of him. The guard came over and asked why I was laughing — nobody else had ever laughed. When I showed him, he laughed too and liked his job better, I hope.

I didn't have to do the whole Metropolitan the way my family had done the Louvre, in a trot. I lived in New York. The Met was my local museum. I didn't even have to walk until I was exhausted. I could go

down and get a whiff of the Rose Hip and ask
Sharon what she wanted for dinner.

* * * * *

I looked through the Rose Hip's door. There was
only one customer, a young blonde woman who was
leaning ardently across the counter to hold Sharon's
hands, the hands that for me were frozen. And
Sharon was letting her, not resisting. Comfortable.
Familiar. I felt sick. I rapped on the glass. Sharon
looked up, looked dismayed, freed her hands, buzzed
me in. Marnie wasn't there.

I said, "I see you're keeping busy."

My rival was excessively beautiful, really
overwhelming, and ostentatiously healthy too, like an
ad for milk. Formidable. I was glad not to be modest
and humble. Even arrogant, I wasn't sure Sharon
would prefer me. Might she not, like the rest of the
world, care more for flash than for simple sturdy
good character? I longed for a zap gun, a
disintegrator. I wanted to vaporize this blonde, not
out of jealousy — I was far too enlightened for
jealousy — but as a good deed, a public service.

She looked at me impatiently, waiting for me to
leave, and then looked again, and once more, and
smiled, saying, "Hi, I'm the Huckleberry Muffin
Queen, but you can call me Candi, with an i."

I didn't know whether Sharon's sudden glum
expression was about me or about Candi, but I
figured either way could work out all right for me, so
I smiled back at Candi.

I said, "I've spent the day at the Metropolitan
Museum."

"I've spent the day at Hunter College, but the Met is one of my favorite places. Really. I really really like art. A lot."

"Tomorrow I'm going to the Guggenheim," I said.

"Me too!" she said. "What a coincidence! It's been on my calendar for weeks! Maybe I'll see you there."

I didn't stay long. I said essentially nothing to Sharon. When I left, Candi came with me, and stood with me at the bus stop.

"How well do you know Sharon?" she asked.

"Hardly at all," I said. Not exactly a lie.

Candi said, "She's driving me nuts. We really had something nice going, and, bam, she wants to quit. Just like that. I'm not used to that."

"It's her loss," I said.

"I don't mean I'm going to mope my life away about her or anything. But why? Why? That's what bugs me. Is it something I did? Something I didn't do? She says she just wants some time to think. What kind of shit is that?"

"Some people do," I said.

"I ask her, is it somebody else? She says no, not exactly. It's somebody long gone she's been thinking about lately. I said what was so great about her, to remember her when you've got the Love Goddess right here? Is there one single thing I don't do? Better than anybody else? You know what she said? You won't believe this. I wasn't even going to tell you. She said, 'She sucked my fingers.' Boy! How's that for sick?"

"Some kind of pervert," I said. "Here's my bus."

The bus was stalled in traffic down the block. There was plenty of time for Candi to put her arms around me, right there on the busy streetcorner. I

hadn't realized liberation had come so far. She would
have kissed me, too, but I bent away, saying, truthful
for once, "You're embarrassing me."

"The Guggenheim? Tomorrow? Promise?" she
asked, turning me loose.

"Maybe," I said.

"No, listen, you could make me forget Sharon so
fast —"

"I'll see," I said.

"I don't want to cut class for nothing. Say you'll
be there."

"If I have to be definite, it's no. Maybe some
other time."

"Listen, I'm not just trying to make Sharon
jealous. I know you think that, but I really really like
you."

I kept shaking my head and smiling.

"Y.T.M.O.," she said, whatever that meant.

My bus finally rattled up and swallowed me. I had
a lot to think about. "Something really nice" indeed!
"Love Goddess" indeed! Candi was lucky she was
bigger than I, so I didn't beat her up. On the other
hand, "She sucked my fingers" was pretty good. I
decided to stay with that and let the rest go, and was
as happy as I dared to be while still not knowing
whether it was me or Candi Sharon was glum about,
whether she'd come home after work or go to
Candi's. Cautiously happy.

When I saw Sharon hurrying along in the street
below, I went out to wait for her at the top of the
stairs. She took them two steps at a time and at the
fifth-floor landing came in sight, very pink and dewy,
so vital, long-legged, healthy and serious.

I smiled hello but she didn't. She was frowning up

at me with a serious intent, as if she were rescuing
me from a fire. As serious and determined as that,
but breathing easily, unlike me. I think she was less
winded from racing up all those flights than I was
from watching her do it.

Before she could reach me, I went back inside to
catch my breath. Immediately I felt her behind me,
her arms reaching around me and her light breath
moving my hair.

"You're here! You're here!" she said.

I leaned back against her. Her body felt so warm
and solid, really there. I said, "Of course I'm here."

"I was scared you'd go home with Candi."

"Why would I go a thing like that?"

"Oh, cause you might be lonesome."

"Not that lonesome."

"Cause I've been mean to you."

"No you haven't."

"No, listen, I know how I acted. Like I didn't
want you, when I did."

"It's all right. I knew you did. I thought you just
forgot."

"I didn't want to get into it again, and then your
folks have a fit again, and away you go again."

How unfair! I turned to face her, still inside her
arms, and said, indignantly, "We were children then.
What was I supposed to do? I wouldn't do that now."

"Don't say you wouldn't. You don't know."

"Yes I do."

"You don't. But I don't care. We can work
something out. If you have any little wishes or
anything, you just come to me and we can take care
of them." She tipped my face up and nuzzled my
cheek, whispering, "You don't have to mess with that

damn Candi." She hadn't forgotten how to play
Whispering in the Ear.

The whisper tingled in my scalp and down my
side. I stayed very still for more. She understood and
kept buzzing nonsense, such as that she guessed
Candi was okay if you liked knockout butch beauty
queens better than plain gray mice from back home,
until the tingles became trembles and my mouth
opened by itself with a groan that meant if you don't
kiss me I will break apart, so we had to lie down
right where we were, on the bare wooden floor,
because Sharon's knees were gone too, and we held
each other in all our sweaty clothes, close enough at
last, mouth to mouth full-length and quiet. So wild to
be joined, so calm then. A mystery.

"I didn't forget," she said. "How could you think
I did?"

We had become so beautiful. We couldn't stop
looking at each other. I believe we had for the first
time our true essence faces, as different from our
humdrum daily faces as stars are from mud.

After a long time, I said, "It would only take one
second to get to the bed."

"Or less," Sharon said.

"Let's."

"Okay."

But we found we were stuck together with sweat
and tears and spit, not knowing which was whose,
and every time we tried to get unstuck, by even an
inch, our bodies rushed back together, gasping and
coming, a delicious problem we were in no hurry to
solve even though it would make everything very
difficult.

For instance, we would have to get a whole new

wardrobe — jeans with four legs, ponchos with extra-big neck holes — and take turns walking backward. And did Chicken Delight make deliveries to sixth-floor walkups? More urgent, did they take I.O.U.s?

We stayed on the floor considering all these problems with no distress, our bodies snuggled together and calm. But there was another problem and it could possibly distress her. Now, while she was still incapable of finding anything bad in me, seemed like the best possible time to mention it.

I said, "Darling, there's something I should tell you."

CHAPTER FOUR:
Sharon

Right away my hammy mind got scared Patricia was going to tell me she was on dope or had VD or she'd bombed a recruiting office or God knew what.

I guess she saw she had me scared. She changed the subject.

"I don't really like the sexual revolution," she said.

I just hung on and waited.

"It seems to have a rule against really caring."

"Seems to," I said, trying to look like I knew all about that, like I'd tried it all and got sick of it a long time ago.

She said, "I know it's exciting, at least as an idea."

"Sure is," I said. I'd probably been excited about Candi, but I couldn't remember why or how it had felt. And when was Patricia going to come back to the point?

She said, "I know it's dangerous to get tied up with one person, because if you lose her where are you?"

I said, "Yeah, that's what happened to Marnie. Her person ran off to some ashram, and now Marnie just lives alone and sleeps with her friends sometimes, and she says she likes it best like that, no big highs, but no bad times. I mean, no horrible times. Of course she has bad. But no horrible."

Patricia said, "I know the old ways were very bad. People were bored or choked-up or lying or fighting all the time. It's right to try to find something more natural."

"Marnie says lovemaking can be friendly. She slept with somebody once that had a hysterectomy, so she thought she couldn't anymore, so Marnie slept with her to show her it was okay. I really like that."

"So do I. For Marnie. But, darling, I want to *love*. I want the walls between us to fall and fall the way they have today, and I want our faces to look like they did a minute ago, and I want to say, 'Where have you been?' and 'What took you so long?' and know the answer won't hurt me and you won't be angry at being asked."

"Of course I won't," I said.

I wished I could say 'darling' the way Patricia could. But it would sound funny coming from me, like belovèd.

And I wished she'd hurry up with her confession while I still had some chance of backing out if I didn't like it.

"I don't want —" she began. She was going very slow so I figured we were back to the hard part. "I don't want us to —" And she stopped again and actually got up and walked around, so I got up too. We were that uptight and not stuck together after all.

"— sleep with anybody else."

If a simple thing like that took so long, how would she ever come out with whatever it was?

I said, "Okay," still waiting for her bad news.

Patricia came back to me. We fit together so nice. Tall and short can be a really nice fit.

"I want to be devoted," she said.

"Sure," I said, still waiting, but then all the worry went out of her body and her face got that pure beautiful look again, so I finally saw.

I'm dumb a lot.

We laughed, and this time we didn't fall down till we got to the bed, which doesn't hurt your elbows like the floor when you want to lean above somebody and watch her be an angel, and doesn't hurt your knees when you're examining somebody who hasn't had a complete physical in years and really needs one.

She was in better shape than she deserved, silky or downy or crisp or slippery in all the right places, and put together so neat, every part an exact fit with every other part. The way her side dipped down to be her waist and then took quite a sharp angle and

flared up again to be her hip put me into such a
trance I lost track of everything else for a while.
When I looked up, I saw she was in the same trance
from watching me. I'd seen that trance face on Mama
when my sisters were babies. On Mama, it made me
jealous. On Patricia, it was for me.

"I'm admiring your hip," I said. "Look at it."

She wouldn't. She said, "I'm not impressed."

"I am," I said. "I think it takes a very smart hip
to look like that." She didn't pull the sheet over it
or ask me to quit, so I think she sort of agreed, right
then, in that trance, even though later, sometimes,
she'd say she was fat and I was prejudiced when I
said no, she was just a different type, a lovely,
beautiful different type. She's just built a little closer
to the ground than some people approve of these
days, and has short solid legs and arms, and little
blunt squarish hands and feet and nice big ribs, quite
far around.

I nudged her breast out of the way with my cheek
and kissed her ribs, which were all wet from where
her breast kept the sweat from drying. It smelled like
cherry juice or raspberry jello but tasted like
rainwater with a trace of salt.

She said, "I feel like a sea anemone fully
expanded," so I left my mouth there a long time, and
then I put my ear against her belly and heard her
innards gurgling gently away. I listened to her heart
going ker-dunk, ker-dunk, so strong and steady, not
very fast, not wild or anything. Strong and steady
and calm.

She said, "I used to hold my breath underwater
as long as I could. It was good practice for now,
because I forget to breathe."

She said, "There's a place in Greece, a very holy place, called Delphi, and I feel we're there. I mean, suspended above it. Like eagles."

I wanted something that good to say back at her, but all I knew was, "I love you. Patricia, I love you," and I guess it was enough.

I woke up in the dark, but New York is never really dark and there was also a big full moon shining through the window. Patricia woke up too as soon as I moved away from her, but I was thirsty and had to pee, so I had to be tough, and of course she needed the same, once she woke up and knew it.

Afterwards we stood at the window and watched the moon heading down the southwest sky, turning the poor old tenements silver and us too. The regular bums and weirdos were out, plus some extras who probably could have slept if the moon hadn't stirred them up and tugged at them. Every once in a while one of them would let out a yawp, sort of a spooky yowl that started low and went high and stayed high and echoed, and then another one would join in to keep it going, and then another one would, until finally they'd have enough and quit for a few minutes. I figured it must be love they were howling for. I felt so sorry for them because they wanted to be eagles above Delphi too, but couldn't.

I also wished they'd shut up before Patricia started thinking the neighborhood might not be too good. Being a New Yorker, I wouldn't have noticed them, same as I never noticed fire trucks or pneumatic drills or stuck car horns or burglar alarms, but Patricia was from out of town.

But I guess nothing could bother her right then. She leaned back inside my hug, her head under my chin, and said, "You know why they're yelling? Because they're made of ocean and it's high tide. We're all little oceans held up by skin."

I said, "I know. I heard it sloshing around inside you."

She said, "We're each zillions of tiny sea animals smooshed together, that figured out how to walk around and bring the ocean along. And when the full moon pulls the big ocean, it pulls our little ones too and makes us howl."

Patricia was sure lucky to have me. Somebody else might have thought she was nuts, but I knew she was playing. I loved how she played in her mind like that.

So I didn't argue or say bullshit or try to pin her down on why nobody but a far-out kook howls at the moon. Most people don't. *I* didn't, even in Mote when I thought I'd never see Patricia again and I had nobody but Grandma, but I came damn close. And Grandma, far-out kook or not, didn't either, and weren't we oceans?

But I didn't say that to Patricia. I didn't want her to stop thinking up theories and telling me about them, no matter how shaky and far-fetched they might be. (Once she told me the flying saucers are flown by whales and dolphins out exploring, and the proof is, everybody reports a greenish light from the portholes. "Obviously, they're aquariums," Patricia said, and I didn't say bullshit then, either.)

It would have been only fair for her to be as nice back at me when I said something you couldn't prove in a laboratory either, like that the two of us have been born and born and born for each other. That night standing in the moonlight listening to the bums was the first time I felt sure we had.

"We used to stand in the mouth of our cave like this and listen to the apes howl," I said.

"Uh huh," she said, with a little edge I didn't notice until I pieced everything together afterwards.

"No, really," I said. "I'm trying to remember if we were apes too at the time."

"Sharon," she said, "one reason I love you is you're smart. If you're not, please don't tell me."

That wouldn't have hit me so hard, maybe, if I hadn't been sort of skinless right then — a sea anemone fully expanded. I pulled away from her. There was a big sweaty slurpy smacking noise when my belly came away from her back. I wandered to the bed and flopped down. Patricia followed me, saying, "Darling, darling, don't let me make you look that way!" and "Darling, I didn't mean it!"

She gave me a corner of the sheet to blow my nose on and kissed my tears away and went on to kiss and pet every single part of my body, some I didn't know I had until her mouth and hands woke them up and thrilled them, and I felt her love protecting me like an ocean, I mean a safe place to be a sea anemone in, but I fell asleep knowing she did mean it, did mean nuttiness was her turf and I was supposed to make sense all the time. I was too happy to care, and sure, in fact, that I could manage. I knew I could be smart every minute of the next hundred years.

* * * * *

In the morning, Patricia pretended to stay asleep, so I could get up. I did carry my cup to the bed and squat there admiring her while I drank my coffee, but I didn't touch her or get back in. Then I bathed away our mixed-together yummy smells. I hated to do it, but I didn't want strangers on the street getting the hots for me. I put on fresh soft clothes that felt like a hug because Patricia had taken them to the laundromat for me.

My bus was full. I had to stand, and when my hand reached for the strap and passed my nose, I caught a light whiff of Patricia, very faint, just a trace, still on my hand in spite of soap and water, like a gift.

I'd never heard of anything as wonderful and interesting as that, so I told Marnie. I didn't expect her to be as overcome as me, but I thought she'd like to know. If I had something original to add to her lore, I figured I owed it to her after all she'd done for me. Anyway, I couldn't stop myself.

"I washed my hands, but she's still on them, a little," I said.

Marnie didn't believe in coffee, so she wasn't quite awake. It takes an awful lot of roasted wheatberry infusion to do what one sip of coffee can do. She even yawned.

"That's why we wear rings," she said. "Under a ring it doesn't evaporate. You can move the ring a little and sneak sniffs all day."

That Marnie — what a know-it-all! If Columbus told her he'd just found America, she'd say, "Oh, we find a couple of Americas a week." I liked her, but she really was a know-it-all, and more about sex than about geography.

But I had to excuse her. Otherwise I couldn't have spent the day explaining how perfect and beautiful Patricia was and how life doesn't need to be sad or hard, and sniffing my hand, which soon smelled, I admit, like carrots and mint.

All in all, Marnie was nicer than most people would have been that didn't believe in love. She didn't tease me or tell me to lay off, even when I scolded her for letting a couple of disappointments make her bitter. Life without love and a mate, I said, was empty and boring, more like walking in your sleep than living. I was really out of line, but the worst Marnie did to me was that one little yawn at the beginning, that I blame on the roasted wheatberry infusion.

After work, I found out why New Yorkers are always in a hurry — they're rushing to their lovers. I rushed, but Eighth Street was clogged-up and so slow the bus couldn't. It finally clunked me to my stop. My sandals hit the sidewalk already running, but stopped, like frozen, when I heard Patricia call my name. She was sitting on somebody else's stoop.

"We've got a table," she said.

I was a little mixed up anyway, from seeing her when I hadn't expected to, and I couldn't figure out what she was talking about. Had Sears delivered a table by mistake and she couldn't wait to tell me?

She said, "I've been guarding it."

Then I saw the table. It was standing slanty on

three loose legs among the garbage cans where some sensible person had thrown it. It was very cruddy with greasy grayish dirt. Why had anybody kept it for one minute ever?

But Patricia loved it. "It's cherry," she said. "It's a Queen Anne library table. I was afraid I'd have to fight somebody for it, but you came in time."

She was like a dog that thinks everybody wants his icky spitty old ball.

She said, "In a population this big, I might not be the only one with eyes to see."

I said, "It's lost a leg."

"No, the other leg was in a garbage can. It's not even broken. It's still got its bolt. All it needs is a nut."

Well, the fact is, I liked things nice. I liked things *new*. Which was why my place was empty. I liked it better empty than filled with anything I could afford, or, my God, trash from the street.

Patricia said, "When I walked past it, it said, 'I am your Grandma Moses table.'"

Hadn't she just said it was Queen Anne?

"It said, 'I'll help you be a genius.'"

If I'd said a table talked to me, she'd have put me on probation right away, but I kind of enjoyed getting one more chance to be the finest and fair-mindedest person around. Patricia always gave me a lot of those chances. Fairness was never her best thing.

I looked at her very kindly, hoping she'd copy my example someday if *I* was foolish, and there was her face with some of our lovemaking beauty still in it and her eyes wet and sparkly brown and her mouth soft and pink and happy, and my whole insides just stopped.

"You want it, darling?" I asked. I actually said darling, like I thought I couldn't. It was easy, even with dozens of people passing by. I actually said, "You want it, darling? Okay," and picked up one end of the table.

She laid the fourth leg on top, picked up the other end, and away we went, me in front, walking backwards and twisting my neck around to see, because I was stronger. She was pretty strong too, though. I was surprised at how she hung in, and always let me be the one to ask for a rest.

We had a block and a half to carry that thing. It was heavier than its curved legs and general unsquareness made it look. Patricia said the weight came from the fine wood, which she would make beautiful again, don't worry, but she mainly saved her breath for carrying. One nice thing, everybody got out of our way. Afraid they'd catch something awful, I suppose.

I kept waiting for Patricia to laugh and say she was kidding, she was just seeing what ridiculous thing she could get me to agree to.

Then we had five flights to rassle that thing up, me on the low end because I was stronger.

At last we stood the table in its place between the two front windows. It didn't look any better. While Patricia gazed and gazed at it, I ran us some bathwater.

We dropped our filthy clothes in a heap. Together we got into the big old bird-footed tub in the kitchen and washed each other's crud and sweat away with soap that left the smell of lavender on us.

I loved how Patricia washed me, so quick and businesslike, the way a nurse would maybe, or a mother checking your nose for boogers. A really practical bath she gave me and finished by scrubbing my knuckles and the soles of my feet with the fingernail brush. I almost said, "Don't stop!"

But she put her finger over my lips. "Don't try to make anything last, even the most delicious," she said. How did she know that?

It was all over in a couple of minutes, and sexier than being slow and teasy would have been. I was noticing and remembering everything my body liked so I could do the same for hers. I mean, *every*thing, not just what Patricia did. For instance, my body liked the vibrations when I stood over the rear axle of the bus. I hadn't quite figured out a home version of that, but I was working on it. And that night I learned that being tended in a no-nonsense, no-games way was the best game and that you shouldn't try to make anything last, no matter how delicious.

Some people think natural instinct is all you need, but I think you need to pay attention too. I wished I'd paid closer attention to Candi. Of course Patricia wouldn't have let me do anything she knew I'd learned from Candi, but I didn't have to tell.

I just wanted to know more, without asking. I sure didn't want to say, "Tell me what you like," or ask her, "Was it good?" What if she said she liked something and I did it and she didn't like it after all because she kept thinking the only reason I was doing it was because she'd said she liked it? I figured paying attention was my best bet. I trained my skin to listen to what was happening in her, and I also bought a couple of paperback sex manuals, which were for straight people but our erogenous zones (what a coldhearted way to put it!) our erogenous zones turned out to be the same as theirs — all the places where one kind of skin turns into another kind, like between the hairy and unhairy sides of your arm, like the crinkly outside of your lip and the smooth wet inside, and all holes, including nostrils, but watch out not to block her air. The sex manuals also had various good advice I like to think I could have worked out for myself, such as never touch her pips without clean hands and short fingernails, and don't dig your elbow into her breast.

One thing I remembered about the time with Candi was how much she wanted me to come, how if I didn't she got all depressed and guessed she was a lousy lover and so on, to make me feel guilty. She almost made me mad enough to leave her even before Patricia showed up. Talk about oppression! So I knew not to act like that with Patricia. Whether Patricia and I come or not doesn't matter. I can't even say it's better when we do.

Candi would never have bothered with nostrils. They feel wonderful, but they don't knock your socks off.

Letting Patricia know about those books might have made her feel funny, like asking how she wanted to be touched, so I kept them at the Rose Hip and read them there, even though Marnie was sure to think it was funny how dumb I was. She did flap through them once, saying, "Couldn't you find one by a woman? What do men know about women? Women always lie to men."

She handed the books back. "Never mind," she

said. "Learn from everybody. Even men. Even cats. Especially cats."

I said, "I was afraid you'd tease me."

"Oh, no," Marnie said. "I've always been an eager student in the School of Desire myself. Whenever I flunk out, I immediately re-enroll. In that one area, you could say I'm an education bum."

I didn't know what "education bum" meant. She had to explain it's an old-timey expression for somebody who can't stop going to school and gets degrees and more degrees on and on.

I decided I wanted to be one of those, of course only in the School of Desire.

CHAPTER FIVE:
Patricia

My table took me three days, one to scrape it down to the bare wood and sand it, one to let the stain and then the matte varnish dry, one to rub it with fine steel wool and paste-wax it. I thought of Mother the whole time and the many jobs like this I'd seen her do. I felt very close to her. Whatever our differences, we had refinishing in common.

Nice Sharon managed not to say the table looked worse every day or complain that I was sharpening

our only kitchen knife out of existence. If I hadn't
already known she loved me, I would have known
when I saw how she struggled not to hurt my
feelings through all that. I in turn didn't call her a
child of plastic and chrome and high gloss, a child of
Sears.

She had a gene for thinking something old was a
confession of poverty and failure — unAmerican —
and this table was old *and* had cigarette burns and
gouges and ink spills and dents here and there on
top. The legs were merely scuffed-up and scruffy.

"We'll get a tablecloth," Sharon said, kindly.

I always sound most sure when I am least sure.
With generations of schoolmarms in my voice, I said,
"Things are supposed to show the marks of their
lives, the way hands and faces do," even though I
had been working very hard to remove as many of
the marks of this table's life as I could.

Sharon didn't jump on the contradiction. I'm sure
she saw it, but as usual she passed up the chance.
She's so strange. I guess it's because nobody at the
Almo dinner table ever tried to be the Most
Promising Youth.

When I buffed the table, it suddenly looked *too*
good, so silky-ruddy it turned Sharon's head clear
around. The scales fell off her eyes and she saw
possibilities where she shouldn't have, in the
damnedest things, which she labored up the stairs
with and presented to me, like a cat bringing you a
dead bird, proudly. She didn't understand that some
ugly, hopeless, impossible trash is really trash.

At first I was too busy painting to pay much
attention. "Put it in the corner," I'd say, with my
brush gripped in my teeth like a pirate's dagger, and

never take my eyes off my picture. "I can't look now
— I'll lose my light," I'd say. Someday my correct
lamp would come and I could paint all night, but it
hadn't yet.

While the daylight lasted, I'd stand leaning over
my table doing quick little watercolors, like this: I'd
scrumble and scribble around with a light-colored
wash — yellow, say — and then look for what was
hiding in it, as images hide in clouds or wallpaper
stains or ink blots or the heads of trees, and when I
found something I'd bring it up with strong bright
colors and wow! a painting! I did so many fish
pictures I almost got worried.

But I'd seen a documentary of Aristide Maillol
standing among his all-but-identical nude sculptures
of young women. He was feeling stale. He had to
walk and walk, getting refreshed, getting impressions.
His head snapped up. His eyes snapped open. He
rushed back to his studio in great excitement. He
began to work feverishly on a new piece, a nude
young woman.

Thanks to Maillol, I knew you could repeat
yourself a lot and still be well thought of. So I didn't
really worry about doing so many fish, but I was
relieved anyway when they got legs and became birds
and angels, and then more legs and became flowered
cats. In a few weeks I had a nice stiff rattly stack —
I used fine hand-laid paper — and I was ready to
mat my pictures and take them to market. I was
ready to sit down.

That's when I took my first good look at the junk
Sharon had brought home. A gilded ballroom chair
with a snapped-off back, badly designed, unfixable. A
pseudo captain's chair with all its back spindles out

and their sockets clogged with hardened glue. Someone trying to fix it had raced the glue and lost. (After an experience exactly like that, Mother threw away her glue gun. "Lest I forget," she said.)

Luckily Sharon had also brought home a milk crate for me to pad and ruffle into a footstool someday in my spare time. It was too low for sitting at the table, but just right for gazing. I cut my mats, pasted the top edges to the backs, slipped the paintings in. I lined them up along the wall and gazed and gazed.

Could I possibly, little me, have created them? But wouldn't it be even more arrogant to think something divine had chosen little me as its channel? Finding a standpoint was a fascinating problem. When combined with gazing, it was hypnotic.

The spell was broken by the slow thumping of something heavy on the stairs. Thump. Rest. Thump. Rest. A refrigerator? A boat? I went out to look.

It was a door, an ordinary two-panel interior door thick with paint, chipped, flaking, warped, with Sharon, very red but joyous, propping it up and breathing hard.

"It was in front of an old brick townhouse on *Perry* Street, so it must be good," she gasped.

"You carried it across town?"

"They wouldn't let me on the bus with it. The driver shut the door when he saw me coming."

"You carried it all that way alone?"

"I was afraid if I came home to get you, somebody else would take it."

I suppose in a way I deserved that, but really our cases were not the same. A table with a run of bad luck is not the same as a door, even one from Perry

Street that under all its lumpy paint might be mahogany. What do you do with a door?

"What do you do with a door?" I asked.

"I thought maybe a coffee table?" she said. Timidly. I hate it when she's timid. Am I so harsh she can't speak up?

I was reasonable. "But it's got doorknobs," I said.

"You'd take them off?"

"Then it's got a doorknob *hole*."

"Oh."

"Darling," I said, "if you want to make a coffee table, please do."

"Uh," she said.

"Go ahead. I'll love it. You'll do a great job."

"Uh," she said, and went silent. She didn't admit, then or ever, that I was the one who was supposed to hassle that door. Sometimes it's okay when she's timid. Sometimes it's appropriate.

That door, along with another one much like it, became our bed. We laid them side by side on milk crates and put the mattress on them and had a bed worthy of our beautiful love, as well as a soft seat the right height.

We spent a lot of time there, but little by little we became able to pull our noses out of each other and look around and wonder what the rest of the world was doing. Had it missed us? Better go see!

Sharon didn't want to go to Ap-Foo, A Place for Us. She was afraid the Huckleberry Muffin Queen might be there. Seeing her might be sticky, Sharon thought, but I liked the idea. I really wanted to see

Candi's face when I walked in with Sharon, and especially when I walked out with Sharon. I planned to be cool and not say, "Now who's the Love Goddess?"

So we decided to go to Ap-Foo. Candi was hardly ever there. She came only to cruise and stayed away when she found somebody. In a few weeks she'd be back, too busy coming on to somebody new to bother us for being finks and letting her make a fool of herself. Being a fool wasn't something Candi brooded about, I think.

So Sharon stopped worrying about Candi and began enjoying Ap-Foo. I enjoyed it from the start, one way or another. Just being in a room with thirty or forty lesbians was an enjoyment not to be sneezed at, and usually there was something more, a panel discussion of Butch and Femme: Myth or Reality? or a speaker to agree with or resist.

Once some female-to-male transsexuals came to tell us how to get operations and become men, just assuming we longed to, and what an uproar our women made, crying, "I don't *want* to be a man, I want to be a *lesbian!*"

Once a shrink came and said society would accept us if we'd stop using loaded, antagonistic words like "lesbian," and we said that word tied us to a community of free women on the Isle of Lesbos and we loved it and we didn't have to adapt to a creepy old world that was wrong about everything and fast dying away.

Once some couples came who were married women with their live-in companions. I mean, the companions had moved into households that had husbands and children around, and lived that way for years, as

permanent guests and servants and, with luck, lovers.
We didn't yell at them. They made us too sad. Their
message was, "You can be quite unhappy doing it
this way." The interesting thing about them was that
in each case the live-in companion was conventionally
feminine and the wife/mother was a stone butch in
full drag.

Sometimes someone would play her guitar and
sing us love songs with the pronouns cleaned up, all
she and her.

And one time who came was Noel Hayes, my dear
old Noel, who had finished her book about how men
think that if they can bury women deep enough they
can get rid of all the evil in the world. The book had
made Noel famous and she made lots of money
lecturing, but she came to us free, saying, "I should
have been here a long time ago, but I was too
chicken."

We were all proud of Noel, the American Simone
de Beauvoir, risking a brilliant career to stand with
us. She said the success of lesbian liberation, gay
liberation, was inevitable, because it wouldn't make
any difference, even in the birthrate — in the whole
world, nothing but our suffering would be changed —
but women's liberation was a real revolution, a real
overturning, which would change everything,
everything. Work, property, government, domesticity,
environment, everything. Women's liberation would
take a while. It would be powerfully resisted.

"So usually," Noel said, "that's where I put my
energy. But tonight I want to be with you."

Sharon was glowing at Noel, so I thought it
would be all right if I did. I did love Noel. I did. How
had I forgotten?

Then Noel said, "I like to sleep with my friends, and I happen to have a lot of friends," and while I was remembering, with, I suppose, a foolish smile, how great it had felt to be a one-way Stone Age mythical butch while she cried, "Oh, Patricia, you are divine!" and wondering if she needed one more friend, Sharon looked at me and I remembered that I was the one who insisted on faithfulness. I made the sweeping finger-snap gesture that means, damn, you've missed your bus, and smiled at Sharon. When the rest of the crowd left, we did too. I didn't join the women around Noel and ask, "Remember me?" It wasn't hard. I really do insist on faithfulness.

Sharon phoned the women she called "The Mothers" from the Rose Hip and got us invited to go walking with them. They were working their way through the New York City guidebooks, one point of interest per Sunday, with the end nowhere in sight, like reading the encyclopedia, and the Bronx Zoo was next. I doubted that the zoo was just naturally next. It was too perfect a place to take the children. I detected condescension.

Sharon said, "I want to see the kangaroos jumping along."

"Why? You gots *me!*" I said, executing leaps that were simply amazing for starting cold. I impressed myself, but because I didn't have a baby sticking out of my pocket, Sharon held out for the real thing.

She was excited and happy because she was about to give her darling Mothers and her darling me to each other and watch us be overjoyed. I was willing to be pleased but had my doubts, which were only increased by Sharon's enthusiasm. The more she burbled about them, the more the Mothers seemed likely to be yucky-sweet, or Good Sports, or Modern, or Wise, or Outspoken, or Young at Heart.

And yes, they were all that, but who's perfect? By the time the afternoon was over, I didn't care.

The zoo was great. It had African crowned cranes running free all over the place, like pigeons. From then on I didn't feel right about a painting until it had at least one tall bird with a sunburst on its head tucked in somewhere.

The kangaroos stayed in their house. We didn't get a glimpse of them.

A giraffe peed an eight-foot-long cascade.

We saw a lesbian couple with a child who called the butch Daddy.

There were tiny antelopes called duykers, pronounced dikers, that Mother One decided should be the national animal and mascot of the Isle of Lesbos. She said she was having to give up the idea of buying Lesbos as our homeland because she saw all the trouble the Jews were having with theirs. We'd have to have an army.

"Oh, let's anyway!" Sharon said.

Mother One said no, Manhattan was also an island and a good home for us — but the duykers did make her start to hanker again. They were so little and they were named for us. We should have our own country and keep them as pets. Every household in Lesbian Nation could have at least one, and our friends would tell us duyker stories instead of cat and dog stories, what a relief!

Of course that was all on the cute side, but I was deciding not to mind. I was deciding to feel superior. And just as I was really enjoying my lack of cuteness, Mother Two caught my eye. Fraternally. Amusedly. Butch to butch. As if to say, listen to the silly little things prattle, isn't it pretty?

Maybe I was already thinking something a little bit like that, maybe I was, but I never would again. Mother Two shocked me out of it. How could she condescend to the one who had given her a seat at life's feast?

I guess you can't see a fault in yourself until you see it in someone else. Even though I could really perfect myself by seeing a lot of Mother Two, was it worth it?

But she redeemed herself at the elephant, a very huge elephant standing behind a stone wall and reaching across another stone wall to the people. His trunk barely reached. I suppose the zoo people measured it before they built the walls. He held it straight out except for the tip, which was turned up to form a permanent begging bowl.

We bought official elephant food out of a vending machine, little cellophane bags full of brownish cylindrical pellets, and waited our turn at the elephant. There was a crowd around the tip of his trunk, a lot of parents encouraging and children sensibly holding back. They ended up dumping their pellets on the wall.

I expected to be much braver than mere children, but up close that elephant was an impressive beast and his eye in its rings of gray wrinkles looked rather alien, rather *other*, not really cuddly. His

enormous nostrils were flared open. He breathed
through that trunk. Might the pellets go to his
lungs?

While Sharon and Mother One and I were
discussing whether to give our elephant food to
someone else, up stepped Mother Two like a
symphony conductor, like a surgeon, unhesitating,
confident. Our sturdy little hero with a heart that
had never known fear and a hand that had never
faltered.

Up went that steady hand, down dribbled the
pellets into that vast snout, and the elephant with
one whoosh sucked in all the pellets and the
cellophane bag too, simply inhaled them. That made
Mother Two grab back her hand and yell a sincere,
innocent, plain-scared yell, and she didn't get angry
when we laughed, and she laughed too, and I saw she
wasn't so bad after all, not so very touchy and
condescending and butch-chauvinist after all, not too
proud to scream.

We waited for our so-called subway high above the
street on a platform that swayed and creaked like a
tree. "It's okay. It always does this," Sharon bragged,
proud of knowing the city, in detail, from her earlier
career, but I clung to a post anyway, knowing very
well it couldn't save me but unable to let go. My
fingers could never be pried loose. The post and I
would have to be buried together.

Mother One and Sharon were strolling around
conceitedly, looking out across the Bronx and
chatting. If I hadn't been so scared, I would have
liked to catch Mother Two's eye and see if she'd like
to share a little smile at their expense. She had a

drowning grip on a post, too, showing once again she wasn't too proud to do the right thing.

Long before we saw the train coming, we felt it. Its hugeness seemed certain to bring us all down. The platform went crazy, but held up one more time. Pretty soon we were back in Manhattan safe underground where subways belong and breathing easy.

Sharon wanted to talk, but I hate talking on subways, shouting and saying "What?" That's where the New York accent that goes through you like a drill comes from. It's pitched to carry. All right, but we didn't need to be assimilated that much. I shook my head to shush her and looked away.

So by the time we were up on the street walking home, Sharon had been bottled up a long time. I couldn't have shushed her then if I'd wanted to, which I didn't. I liked almost everything she said.

She said, "Don't you want to know what Mother One and I were talking about while you two were hugging those posts? You were so funny."

That's the part I didn't like as much as the rest.

She said, "Mother One thinks I should go back to school. Do you think so? She says the city college is free. She says it's pulled generations of slum people and immigrants out of poverty, and that's what I am, she says. Do you know what she called me? An unlicked cub! 'Pretty much an unlicked cub,' she said. I wondered, should I be mad? But I think she meant it okay. 'Pretty much an *immigrant* unlicked cub,' is actually what she said. Just because I come from America doesn't make me not an immigrant. What am I going to do, she says, clerk in that dinky herb store all my life? Should I tell Marnie she called it dinky? She said, Mother One said, New York takes all the people the rest of the country is scared of, like blacks and Hispanics and Asians and queers, and it sends us to CCNY. It used to be Jews and Irish and Italians, but now they fit in and now it's us. She said that if ever New York stops doing that, boy will they be sorry, the rest of the country. Because it keeps us all here together, instead of in their lap, till we're fit for company, she said. Fit for company! What a thing to say! And New York does that generation after generation, waves and waves of us. She says the city is a big rough tired mother, like a mother lion, and sometimes she cuffs us and sometimes she slurps us with her tongue. That's when she said I'm an unlicked cub. As soon as one litter is on its way, bam there's another one. Mother One says this free college system is how she slicks us up, but there's always too many of us. We can't all get in. But I can, because I'm smart, she said. Did I tell you I was valedictorian?"

"You were?" I said, very pleased.

Sharon said, "Well, I was stuck at Grandma's in Mote without a friend, so I read my lessons."

I said, "You were valedictorian!"

"Sure. Why not? But what do you think? Why should I go back to school? What's it got? I mean, that matters? To me, I mean? Do I need to? I'm already an herbalist. Isn't that enough?"

There had always been an arrogance in Sharon, a certain kingliness that I envied and also despised a little. Clerking in an herb store was not the same as being an herbalist. If Sharon opened the door for the President, she'd think she ran the country. The good

side of the trait was that she never complained or
envied anybody or felt like a failure or pitied herself.
When you're competing with just the humble folk
around you, you can feel that way. As for me, I
competed with world history and God and never came
out ahead.

King or not, Sharon could get her feelings hurt,
and I had to think and think how to answer without
calling her an unlicked cub. The gap got long.

"Be perfectly frank," she said.

"You might like to learn more about herbs," I
said, imperfectly frank.

"I'm *studying* herbs, every day, with Marnie."

I thought of how a college would teach herbs, if
at all. A lot of dreary pharmacology. Injecting poor
little critters and then killing them to see what the
injections had done. Statistics.

Then I thought of the Rose Hip, fresh and
fragrant, womanly, and in it a genuine Old Wife
(new-style, but of the ancient line) who was generous
with tales and intuition and knowledge, memory and
imagination.

Yes, woman to woman was the right way to learn
herbs. Sharon would go to school and study
something else.

"There's other stuff," I said.

"Like what?"

My mother always said the only thing her
education had done for her was to make her good at
double crostic puzzles. Was that worth recommending?
Should Sharon study philosophy and wonder the rest
of her life where the desk went when nobody was
looking at it and how it got back instantly when
somebody came into the classroom? (And was there

anything in King Tut's tomb until Carnarvon and
Carter discovered it? Was there, in fact, a King Tut's
tomb at all?) What good would a head like that do
Sharon? Studying American history in college, where
they start to add the bad stuff, might rid her of some
illusions, but she was a good Sixties Baby Boomer
and already believed the worst of us.

"I don't know," I said at last.

"You think I should, don't you?" she said
accusingly.

"I guess I do have a bias in favor of education," I
said.

I had a crop of watercolors ready for market. It
took steely guts to stand with them in Washington
Square and be overlooked. My marketing sample was
big enough — two — to be generalized from. If
Sharon and I loved the paintings, obviously enough
other people would too, sooner or later, but it was
not easy for me to stand there among the other
painters and the folk singers and the drunks and
junkies and not be, usually, even noticed.

Being noticed was almost as bad. I was afraid
that, by some impossible coincidence, word would get
back to the Old Place that a member of the Burley
Family had become a peddler, and an illegal one at
that, unlicensed, practically a Bowery bum. Somebody
we knew would catch me and tell.

Then a straight couple paid me ten dollars for one
of my angels, a beauty with a blue-dotted green dress,
little pink hands and feet, and a golden trumpet. I
thought guilt might wither me before I could hand

her over like that, for *money*, to *them*. What a betrayal! But there turned out to be a Patricia I hadn't known about, a whole new me, sort of sly and fond of money. I took the ten home to Sharon, like a miner pouring his week's pay into his wife's skirt.

"There's more where this came from," I bragged, suddenly afraid of nothing except that I might not be charging enough.

It was fall by then, cold when the sun set. After supper Sharon, looking entirely lovable in her brown and rust and yellow warm soft clothes, would go off to night classes at CCNY. I'd take my portfolio to the square then because that's when the tourists were around looking for something to buy, something to tell about back home.

"Where's the queers? I want to see the queers!" one of them cawed while walking, all unaware, with two of the dykiest-looking women you could hope to see. Their expressions were interesting.

"Here!" I called, smiling, but the woman covered her face and hurried away. Her dykey companions looked at me from behind her back and smiled.

Was she embarrassed about saying "queer?" It's an okay word. It just means "different." I like it better than "gay," which seems too trivial for a matter of life and death. Was she afraid I'd beat her up or rape her? Maybe I did look somewhat powerful. A woman's love shows in your face, and so does money enough to pay your share. But I never meant to scare that poor soul. All I wanted was to sell her a picture. Yes, even her. I would have sold a picture to Richard Nixon, if he liked it.

CHAPTER SIX:
Sharon

Marnie said, "If I were a bright young woman starting out in life —"

(I really hate it when people say that.)

"— I'd become a nonpolluting alternate energy engineer."

(Because I know they wouldn't. They just want me to.)

I was still a freshman. It was too soon to worry about a major. Actually, Marnie wasn't worrying. She was dreaming, for me, to save me the trouble of working up a dream of my own.

"I'd put all the exercise freaks into huge exercise wheels, like gerbils, and let them turn Con Edison's turbines," she said. "I'd catch farts. They're what's in your gas stove, methane."

Marnie was an idea person. Somebody else, such as me, should work out the little details.

"And train wheels generate heat against the rails. Heat and cool the train with it," she said.

Except when she aimed them at me, I did like how Marnie got carried away by thoughts. Once she got interested in some thought or other during dinner, and what with talking and waving her arms, she accidentally ate her friend's dinner along with her own. I heard that from Mother One.

"You know how there's always a wind on bridges," Marnie said. "There must be more than enough power in that wind to light the bridge."

All this called for windmill gestures, of course, but Marnie was making bread, and the sticky dough followed her hands right out of the trough and up and around so if she didn't want to get dough on the walls and in her hair, she had to slow down. A slowed-down Marnie was a pitiful sight, like somebody running in high heels.

"The wind a car makes going fast — that could generate energy to help run the car," she said. She made a careful little swirl in the dough with one finger, but being careful took the heart out of her and she got quiet.

By then I wanted her to keep dreaming at me. I *am* hard to please. She had me interested. Doesn't everything start as an idea in somebody's head? Doesn't it always seem nutty at first?

I said, "I do know people have to stop wasting and start taking better care of the earth. And better care of each other, too. We don't need all this stuff."

She said, sadly because she was handcuffed by the dough, "I don't want to give up FM radio and hot water."

"You can have hot water," I said. "You just can't have it coming out of a pipe in the wall."

I hoped she'd let loose with a dozen ways to run a water heater, but she didn't. I had to stumble on by myself, thinking about taking better care of the earth and wondering if there was some easier way to do it than becoming an engineer.

Could I really study engineering? Did I have an engineer-type mind? I'd been pretty good at math and liked it, in Mote, but what's Mote? I'd heard about a math instructor at CCNY who wrote the problem on the board with one hand and erased it with the other as he went, and then did a few pecks on his calculator and said, "I have my answer. How about you?" Nothing like that every happened in Mote. But I guessed I could do it if other people could, if I put my mind to it, if that's what it took to take better care of the earth.

Then one of Marnie's girlfriends came into the shop. Lover, I should say. Marnie had lovers of all ages and sizes and looks, lots and lots of them. With all those miles on her! And it's not like she was a beauty or anything. It was nice to know lesbians could keep doing that stuff on and on. I mean, she was Mama's age, but what a difference!

Marnie lived alone by her own rules in her monk's cell ("a corrupt monk, of course," she said). She would never be monogamous again, she said, and some of her lovers wanted her to be and were hurt and went away, and some got mad because she wouldn't buy dress-up clothes so she could go to the opera with them, and some wanted her to be only butch or only femme, and some had other reasons, and some stayed.

Her life kind of appealed to me, in case Patricia ever left me, in spite of saying she never would, we don't know, how can we? But until then I liked my life better than Marnie's. It was better to be in love and have somebody who when she puts her hand on your hair you can feel it in your toes, and who when you see her climbing the stairs carrying groceries for your supper makes you think it's no fair to be so happy when there's so much pain in the world.

Anyway, in came this lover of Marnie's, Ann, one of the plainer ones that I liked a lot because at Christmas time she had come into the shop crying. She'd met a little group of gay people, maybe seven, with a Gay Pride banner at the corner of Eighth Street and Sixth Avenue and when she asked them what they were going to do, they said they were going to try to carry their banner the length of Eighth Street, join us!

Ann cried then because she didn't have the guts to join them, but this day she was cheerful, like gutless was okay after all. She kissed Marnie a nice hello kiss, which I watched because we never get to see that in the movies or anywhere, and she said, "Look what somebody gave me on the street. Why me?"

Marnie said, "Why indeed?" She didn't really like to have her lovers look lesbian enough to be recognized by strangers on the street.

What Ann had was a handbill saying there had been a raid on a gay men's bar named the Snake Pit (who'd go to a place called that?) and the police took the customers to the Charles Street Station and one of them who was afraid to be booked jumped out the window and got stuck on an iron-spike fence that the fire department had to cut to get him loose. A piece of iron fence went to St. Vincent's Hospital with him. There was going to be a protest march, the handbill said. Join us!

"Damn!" Marnie said. "They're always getting in trouble and giving us a bad name!"

Which was probably the worst thing I ever heard anybody say. I doubt even Pa ever said anything worse, and I told myself Marnie probably didn't mean it — how could she mean it, about a man who got iron spears in him for being gay? — but if it was a joke, it was the worst joke I ever heard. Then I remembered how she wouldn't go to the Stonewall Riots because it was men's fight, not ours, because we don't do the things they do, and no, they're not our brothers. So maybe she meant it, sort of, and I felt very upset and sad and mixed up, because otherwise she was a really good person. How does that happen?

Maybe Ann had Marnie figured out. "You're just looking for an excuse not to march," Ann said. "Never mind — I'm scared too."

Maybe, to Marnie, it was better to look horrible and heartless than scared.

I was scared too, but I said, "Somebody's got to go. I guess it's me."

Then the two of them started saying awful things, like didn't I know the cops were clubbing college kids for protesting the war, what did I think they'd do to a bunch of queers? Did I really want to get permanent brain damage for something I knew wouldn't make much difference, or maybe any difference at all?

Ann and Marnie said they sure wished they had color TV so they could see me better on the evening news tomorrow, and did my folks have color TV?

Everything they said sank in and made me feel worse, but I knew I was going to go on that march. Because it had to stop, this jumping out of windows. Because we had to start somewhere. There had to be something we would not stand still for.

Back when Patricia wouldn't go to the Stonewall Riots, she promised she would go to orderly demonstrations, but did she remember that?

No. Or if she did, she wouldn't admit it.

But this time I went ahead anyway. I dug out the weird winter hat Grandma had crocheted for me, that I was far too vain to wear usually, and stuffed it with paper to make myself a helmet. I put on extra sweaters, cushiony, to make myself an armor, and headed for Sheridan Square. Because there had to be something we would not stand still for. Because jumping out of windows had to stop.

I'd gone a couple of blocks when I heard "Sharon!

Wait for me!" and turned and saw someone struggling along padded up like a baby in a snowsuit. It was a wonder her arms didn't stick straight out like theirs do. She waddled. Her Navy watch cap, the one she sold pictures in, was padded up high. Luckily it was a cold night in the month of March. I leaned against a lamp post to wait for her and laughed. She was out of breath from racing after me. She claimed I looked sillier than she did, but no one could have.

She said I had forced her to do something stupid and dangerous against her will.

She said I was cutting class for a stupid and dangerous reason.

She said she could be in Washington Square that very minute selling hundreds of paintings.

Then she had her breath back to normal.

"Actually, I do remember I promised," she said.

Sheridan Square is just a tiny triangle where some streets come together at a slant, but I was afraid there wouldn't be enough of us to fill it. We did, though. Mostly men. Patricia flapped through a stack of home-painted signs, like a serious housewife checking out the melons, saying, "Don't you have anything less aggressive?" She finally found one for herself that merely said GAY IS GOOD and one for me that said GAY IS PROUD.

We all stood there being quiet, holding our signs like shields, and then the same young man who passed out the signs yelled, "To the Charles Street Station!" and we walked out in a long thin line, along Christopher Street and Bleecker Street, with people leaning out of buildings or stopping their cars to look, and I thought, what if some of Marnie's

customers see me? What if the old lady I buy the
newspaper from sees me? And all the while I knew
everybody had figured me out with one glance and
didn't care. But I still had to fight with myself not to
be like Patricia, who didn't even work in the West
Village but was hiding her face behind her sign
anyway.

Then the head of the march turned left on
Charles Street while the rest of us were still on
Bleecker, and we could actually see the line while
being part of it. There were so many of us. It was so
beautiful. It was, yes, thrilling. Somebody whispered,
"Look at us!" and Patricia uncovered her face. "Yes,
look at us," she said.

The cops had blocked the street with sawhorses
and their own bodies to keep us away from the
station. The march stopped. Some people in front, not
many, yelled "Pigs!" for a while. That was called
"confrontation." I wished they wouldn't do it. I guess
they figured somebody had to make a noise. Maybe
they thought a protest was no good if nobody
protested. I was mostly afraid they'd embarrass
Patricia so much she'd never march for us again.

The yelling never did amount to much, and the
cops didn't react. Quite soon our confrontation turned
around and became a march again. We gathered
around the main entrance of St. Vincent's Hospital.
Somewhere inside the man who was almost dead from
iron spears was being guarded by cops day and night.
Except for a priest who said a prayer for the
wounded man, we were silent, to show care for him
and the other patients. I felt we were strong then.
The only sounds were the regular New York

noises — subways, airplanes, far-off sirens — and a cop telling his radio he estimated there were two hundred and fifty of us, in good order.

We started back to Sheridan Square. Up comes this scoutleader-type, missionary-type, big healthy woman named Mary, who said she certainly was glad to see some women and next time bring some friends. (Fat chance!) She said she had a small inheritance that made it possible for her to devote her life to winning gay rights. She said she had been marching at Independence Hall in Philadelphia every Fourth of July for years, with nobody noticing, but Stonewall had really made a difference and now we would get somewhere.

She switched between telling us that and yelling whenever somebody started a chant. I could not believe it, but Patricia chanted too: *Say it loud! Gay is proud!* and so on, cheerful, mouth wide open, stomping along Gay Street. I'd forgotten that she was way ahead of me from protesting at college. I tried, but I couldn't get above a mumble.

Patricia said, "These chants are really nowhere. I've been making one up. It goes

Equal and exact
Justice for all people
Of whatever state
Or persuasion."

She didn't have quite enough nerve to chant it all by herself. She just said it.

Mary said, "Interesting. Interesting. Jefferson, right?"

Patricia said, "Yes, and I've got another, all original:

*You've been standing
On my foot for
One thousand years."*

"Interesting. Interesting," Mary said.
I said, "I've got one too:

*It has
Got to stop
This jumping
Out of windows."*

"Interesting. Interesting," Mary said. "There's going to be a meeting. Come and tell them."

The meeting was in somebody's big bare loft south of Houston Street. We filled the sidewalk getting there. We filled the loft sitting in a crowd on the bare concrete floor, listening to that same young man. He said the Ap-Foo officers were so timid they wouldn't even let him use the Ap-Foo Mimeograph machine to put out flyers to protest the Snake Pit arrests, but he and his lover broke into Ap-Foo and ran off the flyers anyway. He said the Mattachine Society was just as inert as Ap-Foo, and the Gay Liberation Front was too Communist. Communism has never been good for gay people, he said. Gay people in Communist Cuba were swimming out to sea in the hope of being picked up by banana boats or the U.S. Coast Guard. He was looking for people and ideas for a new organization that would be active, that would protest and dramatize every piece of homophobic shit that came down, every single one, and nothing else, no side issues.

I would have liked to join an organization like that, but you had to have an inheritance or be on welfare to have time for it. I did enjoy sitting there, leaning against my lover in public and feeling the energy and excitement in the room, like 1776 and the Founding Fathers. Like college life the way other people lived it, all the exciting talk about justice and how things should be, that you miss if you rush to class at night on the subway and rush right back home afterward.

When Patricia and I got back to our place and took off our stuffed hats and extra sweaters, I said, "I guess we didn't need these."

Patricia said, "Oh, but we did. Our march was attacked. Didn't you hear that old man say, 'Take a bath!'?"

We had ourselves a good laugh over that old man — yeah, I heard him too — and how he was the only one who felt mad enough at gay people to say something, and even he didn't put much spirit into it. It was like he had a duty to be nasty to us but no very good idea about how to, so he took what people yelled at the Hippies and made it do.

The war in Vietnam seemed to be ending, sort of — to tell the truth, Patricia and I didn't follow the news too close — but then it turned out Nixon was bombing Cambodia, after saying he wasn't and then, well, yes, but just a little, and anyway he had to. That bombing was no more awful than the rest of that shitty war, but it brought the protesters out again (Nixon called them bums) and four students at Kent State in Ohio got shot to death by the National Guard and some more got killed at Jackson State in Mississippi, and Nixon said, Well, they were asking for it.

We really had to say no to that.

Maybe Patricia couldn't see much sense in gay marches but she did believe in peace marches. Without me even prodding her, she bought us bagels and cheese and oranges and cucumbers and got us two seats on a chartered bus that was part of a long caravan of buses taking people down to Washington to tell Nixon to stop, knowing he wouldn't. To tell the world Americans weren't all Nixons, so we wouldn't go down in history as Nazis and Turks. To make a distance between us and him. To ask forgiveness for America. Those were *our* reasons, anyway. I don't know about the others. They didn't say. The bus was so quiet I could hear the tires on the highway. Everybody was doing their private thing. I think they were praying for America to be forgiven.

Patricia had been in Washington a lot, while her father read at the Library of Congress and stuff like that, but I never had. I was surprised at how beautiful Washington was. How could it be, with all that ugliness going on, men ordering more napalm from Dow Chemical and then going home to play with their kids and eat supper like ordinary sane

people? Well, a rattlesnake seems beautiful too, and
ballerinas on their toes, until you know what they
mean and then you don't think so anymore, and that
goes for Washington too.

We poured off the buses by the thousands and
walked across big grassy spaces, under blossoming
chestnut trees, to the White House, which was
completely barricaded inside a ring of khaki-colored
Army buses packed solid nose to butt. A flea couldn't
have squeezed between them to tell Nixon to stop. He
had said ahead of time he wasn't going to look or
listen anyway. He was going to watch a football game
on TV.

By three in the afternoon the speakers and folk
singers had finished, all without even being able to
get a chant going, and there we were with three
hours before our buses came back after us. We could
go anywhere, the cops said, except Fifteenth Street,
so that's where we went, one hundred thousand or
two hundred and fifty thousand of us, depending on
who you believe, up Fifteenth Street in a huge ooze,
the amoeba that ate Washington, slow and quiet.

I had never been part of a crowd that huge. It
gave me a funny feeling. Eerie. To know we could
stop traffic. To know that nothing we pushed against
could stand. I wanted to turn around and see if
anybody else was feeling it, but I was afraid I'd let
out a stupid giggle and then what would Patricia
think of me? I could see what it must be like to be
in a mob. A mob can do anything and nobody's to
blame, like an earthquake.

But these people were never a mob. Always

separate, doing their private things. The television
crews were there, wishing, I think, we'd be a little
more picturesque. To me, two hundred and fifty
thousand people being quiet are picturesque.

The Communists were making noise, though —
splashing in the reflecting pool, waving their Viet
Cong flags, marching to the Labor Department (which
was closed for the weekend) to "show solidarity with
the working class." They made our serious, solemn,
immense, heartfelt prayer look silly.

"They do it on purpose," Patricia said. "They
want to keep the war going, because it wrecks us."
At Brundidge-Willson College she'd met some
Communists who admitted that.

Patricia and I were partway up Fifteenth Street
when we met everybody else coming back. There was
nothing on Fifteenth Street to do. I guess it dawned
on them that the police told us not to go there so we
would. It was just the most harmless place to be.

And then in all that quiet mass we heard a faint
little chant, "Gay Power to the Gay Gay People!"
and saw about eight people, men and women,
probably the same ones who carried their banner the
length of Eighth Street in New York at Christmas
time, coming down Fifteenth Street with their arms
across each other's shoulders and carrying a banner.

I didn't think Communists should mess up a
serious solemn immense peace prayer by chanting, but
it was okay for gay people to, sort of, a little.
Patricia thought they should feel the spirit of the day
and shut up entirely. For a mostly modern person,

she has a lot of strong opinions about right and wrong. But there were so few of the gay people. How much noise could they make?

We went to meet them. Patricia said, "We want to walk with you. Okay?"

"Sure. The more the better," a young man said.

Patricia said, "But do you have to chant? She can't stand it, and I just barely can."

He said, "I know. It's hard for me too. But we have to," and before he could explain why, a young woman looked at me with disgust and yelled into my face, "Ho! Ho! Ho-Mo-Sex-U-Al!" which was absolutely the worst of all their lousy chants. She picked it to drive us away, I think.

So we walked along the curb beside them but not with them. They had their arms across each other so what did they need with us? They chanted.

I thought they were trying to change the world and couldn't possibly, but no, they were changing themselves. What good is a new world if you don't go into it as a new person? They were squeezing the fear out of themselves. I could see from my own fear what it took for them to face the TV cameras and the dozens of private cameras and the amazed or disgusted faces, but I figured I could have done it too if I hadn't had Patricia grabbing me back. Probably she'd never go on another march, ever. I tried to be pissed at her, and tried not to know I was thankful not to have to be a hero, even though Grandma's cross was commanding me to dare.

The Communists were the only ones that got their pictures on the TV news. The gay people didn't.

That's how it goes. You screw yourself up to come out, and you're not out after all. You have to do it again and again.

Patricia wanted to go up to the Washington Monument where Nixon could look above the buses and see her if he used binoculars. All the way up the little rise the monument is on top of, she was whispering. At first I couldn't make it out, but then I heard it: "Gay Power to the Gay Gay People!"

I still didn't know her very well.

She put her hands flat against the monument and looked down at the White House and Nixon and his binoculars. "I want him to see I'm not a bum," she said.

"What is this?" I asked. "Do you admire him or something?"

"No, I want him to admire me," she said.

I guess if you're silly about your father, a President's opinion means something to you. I didn't care what Nixon thought of me. I would have liked to have him think my mob could push him over.

The road back to New York was lined with cars that had been pulled aside to wait for the traffic to ease up. The buses crawled between walls of little wrecky VWs painted with sunrises and flowers, and people who cheered and cheered us, noisier than they'd been in Washington. Our busload sang "Give Peace a Chance" for miles. Sometimes somebody would get sick of it and start something else, but we always went back to it. Patricia sang in a funny one-note blat, like a little kid, right in my ear, loud, and kind of mixed up my singing sometimes. She said it was alto and thought I liked it. What I liked — loved, in fact — was the little pops and tucky noises her lips and tongue made.

It was around two in the morning when we got back to East Ninth Street, where we felt safe because Patricia was friends with all the street people and they didn't let anybody bother us. Late as it was, she had to stop many times to tell some bum or junkie that we were just back from Washington and feeling good, but tired. She said we were glad we went, and gladder still to be home again.

CHAPTER SEVEN:
Patricia

I worked very hard to make our home beautiful, and it was beautiful — maximally beautiful, I thought — but then Sharon's grandmother sent us an afghan she'd put together for us, because, her note said, at last two somebodies worthy of it had been granted her. She'd been crocheting the squares off and on for years out of every possible dark and bright leftover yarn, each framed in black. We put the afghan on our bed, which was up on its crates and doors by

then, and not just the bed but the whole room moved
up a notch, a whole new level, out of sight. That
afghan just glowed. It seemed to light the room with
color, like a cathedral window.

Sharon was afraid I might think it was not
exactly a Burley Family thing. She thought we liked
everything uncomfortable and brown or gray, but I
loved the afghan. It was art. Even we Burleys think
color is okay in art. I had to admire the afghan
square by square and as a mass, praising her
grandmother's color sense, her boldness, her risky,
unpredictable wonderful effects before I could finally
convince Sharon, *yes,* I loved the afghan.

The middle square was embroidered

P + S
1969

inside a heart, which was the first acknowledgement
anybody in either of our families had given us, and
we felt a mixture of thanks to old Danica Almo and
coldness to all the rest. Aren't families supposed to
wish you well when you set off together, even if
you're illegal and can't put it in the newspaper? It's
true we hadn't been quite forthright, but Danica
knew from our postcard and our history. "Together,
happy, working hard, everything's fine," the card
said, and the rest of them got the same message and
could have felt like shouting Hooray for Love! but did
not.

We didn't know how much we minded until right
then, choked up over Danica's fabulous gift and the

hooray that stuck out all over it. We were surprised. We'd thought all we wanted was for our families to leave us alone.

I was saving up for a good camera, so I could make slides of my paintings before I let go of them. In some ways it's awful being a painter. When writers sell their stuff it comes back multiplied, and musicians have tapes and actors have films. When a painter sells a painting, it's goodbye forever, but slides do help a lot.

Mother Two was very kind about making slides for me, but her camera had parallax problems if she didn't shoot from way back, and the shutter tended to need repair at awkward times, such as after she'd puffed up all our stairs on her little soft legs and was wishing she'd never heard of me.

She was also very kind about buying my paintings, though she looked down on them for being so cheap and on paper instead of canvas. She kept saying I should get a gallery and be serious, never seeing how entirely serious I was and that a gallery would be just like the art department at Brundidge-Willson College, bad for me. If I got mixed up with anything like that again, I once again wouldn't be able to paint.

"For God's sake, be a *pro!*" Mother Two liked to say. To her it was perverse to have a lot of talent and energy but not shoot for the top. Was I some sissy, afraid to compete? Was I an amateur?

Mother One would be laughing, saying, "Shut up, Vera. Lay off, Vera," but I doubt she understood me either.

I still thought it was possible for people to understand each other, so I kept explaining. I'm a pro, I said, because I don't care when somebody looks at my stuff and walks away without saying anything. I'm an amateur, ama-teur, love-doer, because my work is play and not to be adapted to the market by some marketing genius who doesn't love it.

"Well, I do love it, of course," Mother Two, who was a marketing genius, would grumble, "but I don't see why you couldn't do the same thing with oil on canvas."

So I needed a good single-lens reflex camera to get slides without a lecture and without parallax, and just when I had almost enough money saved up, there came this beautiful afghan, a remarkable work of art and love, from Sharon's grandmother.

Sharon laughed and cried, saying, "Good old Grandma!" and "Why's she the only one?"

I said, "Let's go see her."

There went my camera money.

Our bus seemed to poke along, never in high gear, but I guess that was an optical illusion, a parallax problem, because it kept up with the Thruway traffic just fine, and pretty soon we were seeing the Catskills off to the west, low soft rounded-off blue mountains with mist where they overlapped, and they filled my throat and chest like love, like loose homesickness. I was amazed.

What was that about?

The bus left the Thruway at the town of Saugerties and ran along many steep narrow twisty tar roads with little houses strung out along them and gardens tilled and ready for seeds. Much as I loved our dear slum home, I did feel underprivileged right then. I had never minded so much, even when Daddy wouldn't let me go to the Old Place, that the sunny green earth belongs to straight people and we can have only the parts they don't want. It's true we fooled them after all, by making our part the best, but right then I wanted more than beauty and love and bliss and joy. I wanted a garden, too. I wanted trees and a wide bright sky.

Outside Mote, the bus paused and left us — no station or anything, not even a bench, just the roadside, empty except for a pitiful old truck which Sharon recognized and ran to, crying, "Papa Bear! Papa Bear! You're still alive!" It let out a weak honk. The horn was its only quiet part.

In the Burley Family, we *never* name vehicles, but Danica Almo was odd in so many other ways that calling that truck Papa Bear was probably the most reasonable thing she did.

She kept the truck running by petting it and telling it how handsome and strong and wonderful it was. "Trucks are male, don't you think, like dogs?" she said.

During our whole visit, she fed us nothing but bread, peanut butter, and instant coffee for breakfast, and leftover chili out of a huge pot for supper. No lunch.

She said farting is good for you and should never be repressed. She popped away blithe as a baby to set a good example, making a virtue out of what the chili necessitated.

She talked to her tools and her plants and the concrete beasts in her yard, and she talked to the dead. She told me, "Whenever I don't know how to do something, I pick out somebody among the dead who does know and ask them. I say, 'Okay, Grandpa' — he was a carpenter — 'okay, Grandpa, how do I hang this door?' It's all right to ask. You're not crazy unless they answer."

I asked, "Do they answer you?"

"Of course they answer me. Of course my grandpa helps me hang my door."

She said the left hand absorbs and the right hand emits, so you should always keep your right side toward anybody sick or evil, and emit at them, but don't absorb what they're emitting.

There were photographs of her handsome sons in World War II uniforms and beautiful grandchildren of all ages, including some of Sharon I had never seen, jammed together on every surface, but old Danica was not very interested in any of them and couldn't keep their names straight.

She said an unborn child chooses its parents and forces them together. This explains why people who shouldn't spend twenty minutes on the same train together spend fifty years in the same bed, and why all children have a faint lifelong guilt toward their parents. They almost remember.

She was not a Christian and never went to church, but the tunes she whistled were hymns. She gave them a very unstately beat. She said they were folk songs. They were written in the nineteenth century by little old ladies and parsons pumping away at their parlor organs, she said.

There was a grand old Mason and Hamlin organ in Danica's parlor too, but she couldn't play it. It was tall, with mirrors and little shelves for candles and a wide space for hymnbooks. My mother would have loved it.

Poor Sharon was still under the influence of her mother's wall-to-wall beige carpet, despite so many years away from it. She was ashamed of Danica's wonderful house and kept explaining and apologizing, sometimes even in front of Danica. That great rowdy crew of butchy boys wrecked the house growing up. How much could one old lady do alone? What did I expect?

I kept trying to assure Sharon that I loved the house. She didn't see how anybody could, but she did believe I loved her in spite of it, and I was sure a nice person, the nicest person in the world.

We slept in Sharon's old room far upstairs. There was an apple tree solid white with blossoms under the window. We weren't going to make love, because even though Danica treated our marriage as very natural and everyday, we still didn't want to rub her nose in it. I guess nothing is so exciting as trying not to make love. That saggy old bed yelled like a bluejay when the waves hit us, but then it was too late to

care, and I admit I'm never really contented unless
Sharon lets out some cries.

But Danica's bed was far away, and her hearing
practically had to be just about shot, and a mass of
frogs, enough to be a plague, was whooping it up in
the swamp. We hoped they covered us.

Don't trust frogs. The first morning, Danica said,
"I'm glad Sharon's not lonesome up there anymore,"
with a nice smile, without a trace of smirk in it, a
simply human and glad nice smile.

I will say she won me over with how unflapped
she was about us. I had to re-evaluate her. What a
great old babe, in spite of everything! She verged on
wise.

Sharon had years of news for her, so I left them
alone a lot. I hauled mulch, mostly, but one day I
walked to Mote to see the store. I liked stores. They
were a pleasure I could count on. I always walked up
and down the aisles of every one I came to, even if I
didn't want to buy anything.

Mote's store looked charming on the outside, a
really classic barn-red country store, with a front
porch and rocking chairs and, in honor of spring,
plants, not many. A few baby trees in burlap socks.
Some potted flowers. Rosebushes pruned back almost
to nothing, but with pictures of what they would
become on their cartons.

Inside, the store was a letdown. It had a little of
a lot of things, in the great tradition, but hardly
anything on display. Just boxes. You had to know

what you wanted and the clerk would burrow for it. I
tried to be pleased, but that store didn't meet me
halfway. It also smelled mildewy. I had counted on
getting a little high from it. I had counted on
pleasure. I'd had such a reasonable expectation of
stacks of overalls and fishing poles and tractor hats
and monkey socks and printed calico and crochet
hooks and axes and cloth sacks of flour. I felt so
gypped. I went back to the porch. My whole body was
pouting.

Then I saw two wiry old women lifting young
rosebushes onto their pickup truck.

That perked me up. That changed everything.

They looked like lesbians, but country women
often did. Danica Almo did. Any woman with a real
face and comfortable clothes did. I just hoped I did.

I'm not shy, and one of them wasn't either.

I said the roses were sure nice and I bet they had
a nice garden.

She said she guessed it was all right, but a lot of
work, especially roses. They had to be crazy buying
more, she said. Bugs were attracted from forty miles
away, and of course she didn't believe in spraying,
except a little soapsuds for the aphids. Japanese
beetles they picked like cherries and dropped into
alcohol. Instant death, they hoped. Humane.

I said I wished my friend Sharon and I had room
to grow flowers, but we lived in Greenwich Village.

She said she and her friend had lived in the
Village for a while, on Bleecker Street, and
whereabouts did we live?

I said well, actually, it was East Ninth Street, not
quite the Village, which we couldn't afford, but

Sharon worked at the Rose Hip on West Eleventh Street in the Village and I sold my paintings in Washington Square.

She said she had often bought herbal teas at the Rose Hip and catnip for her cats and burdock root for colds. Did that same interesting woman still run it, after all these years?

I asked did she mean Marnie Fellowes or some other interesting person.

She said yes, that was the name, Marnie something, the most interesting person. She said she and her friend had never known anybody as interesting as Marnie, in that particular way, until they moved to New York and they always wished they could make friends with her but it never happened. She guessed they were too shy.

I said she didn't seem shy, and Marnie was very approachable, especially if you had a cold or were constipated or achy. That was the way to Marnie's heart, I said.

She said that was donkey's years ago, and she might not be so shy now. The whole world was changing.

I said yes, even grandmothers were changing. Sharon's grandmother had made an afghan for our bed with our initials in a heart in the center. We had come to Mote to say thank you.

She said if we were going to be around for a while, there was a monthly potluck get-together we might enjoy, some of the interesting women from nearby. She said they sort of tried to stick together.

I said we'd really like that, but we had to leave because Sharon's spring break was over. In case we came again, could I call her?

She said sure. I went back into the store and bought a pad and pencil and wrote down her name, Dot, and her friend's name, Fran, and their address and phone number, and gave them ours, except we didn't have a phone number.

They offered me a ride, but it would have been out of their way, and anyway I wanted to walk so I could look at the world slowly with the new eyes they had given me — now that I knew those little homes, those crotchy apple trees, those barns, those cars, didn't necessarily belong to straights. What a difference! I was all recovered from envy, which had been making me, I saw, sick. I was well and stepping along healthily in a world partly ours, in a light that had taken on a certain gold.

One of our Ninth Street neighbors had been up to the Cape the summer before. She said she had watched a wave slide up over a rock and pull away, and another wave slide up over the rock and pull away, and another wave slide up over the rock and pull away, and another wave slide up over the rock and pull away, and, oh, *God!* it was good to be back in New York.

Oh, God, it was good to be back in New York. I found I had missed black people, I had missed bagels. I liked the country stars, so bright you could read by them in a night so quiet you could hear them crackle, but I also liked roar and hum and endless difference and shopkeepers sitting in front of their grubby shops watching the street and saying hi to us, where you been?

Most of all I liked the beautiful radio stations and crate-wood fires in our fireplace and our own bed and our own bathtub with a hose on its nozzle and Sharon studying or writing, entirely concentrated and intelligent, at our satiny table — all of which had, come to think of it, something in common with a rock and a wave.

I was painting when I heard my name yelled from the street. I looked down and saw Mother Two, alone except for the bright yellow taxi that had brought her, which evidently didn't want to be blamed for leaving her alone on such a street. Ordinarily I would have dropped the key to her, but I called, "Just a minute," and ran down, so I could counsel the cab driver to worry about his own damn neighborhood and keep his filthy paws off mine, which was already in good order, thank you.

Mother Two must have thought I was having a grouchy and aggressive day, because she skipped her usual complaint about our stairs and our lack of telephone. I wasn't grouchy. I was just having fun, and offering a worthwhile moral lesson. People do need to realize it's somebody's *home* they're looking down their noses at.

She went right to her topic, while still following me up the stairs. "We took your paintings to a gallery to be framed, and the woman there was *crazy* about them," she said.

I was pleased but cautious. I set tea water to boil.

Mother Two sat down on the padded milk crate. She said, "Here's her card. It's a nice little gallery on

West Fourth Street. She spread your paintings out
and couldn't take her eyes off them. Really, you
couldn't ask for a better reaction. Little sighs. All
that sort of thing. Quite heartwarming."

"Why did she sigh?" I asked.

"How should I know? Well, it was not in grief, I
can tell you that much. She said, and this is a direct
quote, 'I'd love to represent her.' So there you are,
kid. You've got a gallery. No more standing in that
damn park trying to sell your work."

"I don't *try* to sell it. I *do* sell it."

Maybe I *was* having a grouchy and aggressive day.

"Oh, come on!" she said. "For pennies!"

"I get by. I pay my share. I shave my taxes a
little. Don't tell."

"You haven't got a phone. You live in a slum. I'm
sitting on a crate. What's the matter with you? You
won't always be young. You can't always wear blue
jeans and live on one soybean a day. When are you
going to grow up and take yourself seriously? You
can't always be a kid playing house. Playing lemonade
stand."

It was Mother Two's customary message. I did
wish Mother One had been there to say, "Lay off,
Vera. Shut up, Vera."

I said, "Okay, tell me why she sighed."

"Patricia, listen to me. It is perverse to paint on
paper."

"Good paper lasts longer than canvas. I use the
best. The *best*."

"All right. That may be. But when you know it's
holding you back and you do it anyway, it is
perverse."

I said, "So she gazed and gazed and sighed and

sighed. 'Oh, dear, they're on paper,' she sighed. 'Does she ever do oils?' "

"Right," Mother Two said. "So that rules her out. So you sit here hugging your rags around you like some damned medieval saint, because you're too virtuous and noble to make a good living. Well, enjoy your rags because they're all you'll ever get."

Luckily, summers at the Old Place with aunts had toughened me up. Aunts do like to let you have it right between the eyes, for your own good, someday you'll thank them. And you get used to it and come to understand that they're, in a weird, old-fashioned, idiotic way, showing love. If they didn't love you, they wouldn't bother.

So I didn't get mad. I said, "Maybe you're right. But I have to take it as it comes. I wait for it, like an Eskimo beside a hole in the ice. You see? I can't get tough with it. I can't beat up on it. You see?"

"I see you're getting a little divine flame-y. And I'm getting meddlesome."

"Yup."

"Well, I came all the way down here from my office, by cab, because you haven't got a phone, because I thought I had good news for you, and apparently I haven't. So I'm disappointed. So if I was a little harsh, blame it on that, and I'll say no more."

"It's okay," I said.

"I just don't understand this will to fail. Lesbians have to be excellent. *Excellent!* This flabbiness. This indifference. Just drives me nuts. And I'll say no more."

She almost went too far. Not even an aunt had ever called me flabby. I guess when you're struggling really hard to be courteous to your elder, you can seem flabby and indifferent. She was probing for my fire and ambition. I was giving her pulpy good manners. But wasn't that better than decking her? She was damn lucky that I still bothered with deference to age. I was the last one in my generation to do that.

In June came the first anniversary of the Stonewall Riots, to be celebrated with a great march up Sixth Avenue to Central Park, and of course Sharon wanted us to go. I didn't resist much, even though gay marches and demonstrations seemed useless. If your demonstration demonstrates power-lessness and disunity, what have you gained? And yet *some*thing was changing the world for us. Even up in Mote, Dot and Fran were feeling the change. And maybe the Movement had something to do with it. I didn't see anything else around that might explain it.

We tried to get Marnie and the Mothers to come along. Of course they wouldn't, but they were standing outside a laundromat on Sixth Avenue, pouring tears into their baskets of clean clothes, when the march went by. Out of pity for their poor closety old heads, we pretended not to see them. Their cheeks were really wet, shining, dripping. I think we must have been a touching sight, like the Children's Crusade starting for Jerusalem. Like the Polish horse cavalry challenging Hitler's tanks on the road to Warsaw. I wish I could have seen us.

Afterwards, Marnie told Sharon that what moved

her most was a small, neat, gray-haired woman, a
teacher or librarian, walking by herself in a neat blue
suit and respectable shoes with moderate heels.

Sharon and I didn't see her. We stuck close to the
Ap-Foo banner and brought the Ap-Foo contingent to
nine. I knew from what the other women had said at
meetings that Sharon and I were the only ones there
who actually committed, currently, the acts they were
marching in support of. I doubt I would have gone to
the trouble, myself, for a right I didn't exercise. They
didn't need changes. Nobody was against what they
did. But there they were, unselfishly trudging along.

The men around us were elated and lively.
Marches seemed to energize them. For women,
marching and chanting were just duties. We trudged.

I thought of Carl Jung and his brilliant surmise,
which I never doubted, that it was the task of the
lesbian to save humanity. I kept wishing he had told
us how. But he was very right not to. How could he
know? We'd have to blunder along and find the way
ourselves. Would it be by trudging, or slowly moving
into every freedom and using it and seizing the next,
or by recovering male and female for men and women
both, or what? There was no way to predict. I only
knew we had to head toward such light as we could
see.

And yet — did it mean something that most
lesbians stubbornly and mutely stayed apart from gay
men, the Movement, the great adventure, that there
were only nine of us under the Ap-Foo banner? That
we hated marching? Was weeping on the sidelines
part of our task too?

There were more watchers than marchers, even in
midtown, which was usually deserted on Sundays.

Sharon held up her sign. On it she had painted the title of a very good book, STAND UP, FRIEND, WITH ME. Many watchers read it and caught her eye, seriously, and we knew next year they'd be with us.

The watchers were in no way hostile. Many were weeping. Some were puzzled. I saw some asking the cops who we were and then shaking their heads in bewilderment at the answer. The cops were nice. Only one person in all those miles to Central Park said anything negative, and it was merely something about frying in hell. I welcomed the chance to hold up my sign to someone who would understand. REPEAL THE DEUTERONOMIC CODE! it said. Brundidge-Willson College had been immovable in its belief that an educated person knows the Bible. I yelled, "Judge not that ye be not judged!" (I preferred the King James version. What a majestic ring it had.)

BOOK THREE

CHAPTER ONE:
Sharon

Patricia was so funny. It always took her an hour to walk to the corner grocery because she had to stop and chat with the street people and the shopkeepers because they were all her dear friends. I admit I was glad they all knew us and had watched out for me back while I was still in school and got home late, but *friends?* I think a friend is somebody you do more than chat with, and a whole neighborhoodful of old friends of long standing is something you don't

jump at the chance to get away from, either, without
one look back.

But when I got the lawyer's letter that said
Grandma had wanted to help me in the hard life I'd
chosen and had left her farm to me, and when my
first thought was *sell it,* Patricia said maybe not.

"Maybe we should live there," she said.

"*Live* there? You crazy?"

"Don't you think that's what she intended?"

"Oh, come on! She wouldn't bully me like that.
She wanted me to have some money, is all."

Grandma had run Papa Bear into a tree and died,
just like that. The steering always was sloppy. I think
something finally gave out inside and she lost control.
Sometimes two cars going sixty can crash together
and roll over and over and the people can walk away
with a broken pinky, but hit a tree and you're dead,
always.

Grandma did okay. She never lived with her kids
or in a nursing home, or got cancer or broke her hip,
or any of that awful stuff. She took care of herself,
she was cheerful and curious about life, and as such
things go she had a good end. The only better ways
would be to fall asleep and not wake up — but do
you have a bad dream? — or like President Kennedy,
king of the mountain, cheering crowds, and *boom!*

Grandma had a rotten funeral, though, a lot of
nonsense about self-sacrificing mother, that I could
feel her laughing at. All her customers, for vegetables
and witchcraft and so on, were there, but when I
thanked them for coming Pa whispered this wasn't a
goddamn cocktail party and stop dancing on his
mother's grave. His brothers and their families were
there too, of course. It was kind of eerie to realize

that all these tons of people had come out of Grandma's little body.

Mainly it was nice to see Mama, and my sisters were all grown-up beautiful tall women. Rayanne was part of the oil company, she said, and had her name on the trucks in the form of "and Daughter," which would have been me if I hadn't disappointed Pa. She still didn't know what I'd done. Pa was still mad at me, or mad again because I'd brought Patricia to the funeral, so none of us could talk much. I couldn't wait to get on the bus and see the last of Mote and have my own funeral for Grandma in my heart.

Then came the letter from the lawyer, and Patricia gave me that surprise.

I figured it out in a little while, that she was being nice and saying she'd live on the farm in case I wanted to, seeing as I'd spent my youth there and all, and it might mean something to me, so I explained that all it meant, aside from Grandma, was being lonesome and sad. Patricia said if we were there together, I wouldn't be lonesome and sad, and there were lesbians all over the countryside who got together for potluck suppers. But I must do as I pleased. It was my farm. She would say no more.

Then I got another surprise, from Marnie. I still worked at the Rose Hip while I tried to figure out what my college degree was good for, while I waited for answers to my job applications. Marnie made me describe the farm, which was down to twenty-five acres by then, and said she'd like to take a look at it. She'd like a weekend place. I said it was too far from the city for that, but she said *she'd* decide that.

On the next Sunday, Marnie drove us and the Mothers up to Mote in her tiny car, Mother Two in front with her and the rest of us crunched together in back. Mother One felt nice to crunch up to and sing car songs with.

The trip took five hours. Marnie must have seen she couldn't drive that every weekend, but she didn't say so. We got to Mote around noon.

There was the poor old house gray in the sun. I was a little embarrassed, except that the apple tree was blossoming and looking good, and anyway I'd warned Marnie.

She and the Mothers went all over the house saying, "Look! Look!" with impressed voices, claiming it was a magic house, and beautiful, and just heaven, and then to the barn. Mother One stopped in the doorway and deep-breathed the smell of antique cow manure. She said it was magic too and took her back to her grandpa's barn and she was going to stay right there.

The rest of us went to the fields, where Marnie got all excited, pointing out mullein and· motherwort and comfrey and burdock and purple sunflower. The very herbs we sold by the ounce, like gold, at the Rose Hip, were growing as weeds in Grandma's fence rows. Somehow I had never put it together, like the lady who didn't know she was speaking prose, that Grandma's weeds and Marnie's merchandise were one and the same. Actually I'd never asked about the weeds. They hadn't interested me. And Grandma probably didn't know anyway. Her idea of an herb was parsley.

God, how close people came to losing all that knowledge!

Marnie was pretty impressive poking around in last year's loppy old yellow grass and recognizing even the tiniest new green leaf. Mugwort. Cleavers. Chickweed. Ground ivy. Saint John's wort. I think even Mother Two was impressed, and Patricia almost was.

Then we went into the woodlot, which had never been farmed because it was just one rocky outcrop after another, and extra hilly. The big original trees had been cut long before, but the second-growth maples and beeches were slowly getting big, standing there feeling for cracks in the mossy rocks and filling them and cracking them bigger, slowly, no hurry. But a creek that was temporarily big with spring rain came pouring down from the heights, and it was in a hurry. It jumped down through the woodlot in three little waterfalls and rushed on south between two fields and under the road in a culvert and rushed out the other side, like it couldn't wait to be Catskill Creek and Hudson River and Atlantic Ocean and rain and creek again.

I mean, it was a really nice woodlot, that could have been a comfort to me when I was lonesome and sad before, if I'd thought of it. Sometimes I think I'd never notice anything if somebody else didn't point it out to me.

Here's what Marnie pointed out in Grandma's woods: golden seal, lady's slipper, bethroot, and the champion, the king of plants, which sent her to her knees, ginseng. She let out a yowl that wasn't entirely admiration for the ginseng.

Poor Marnie was at the end of being able to drop to her knees to get a better look at something or admire something, a sad moment, an *important* moment, but Mother Two just laughed when she held out a hand and pulled Marnie up. What was funny about hurting your knees or any of the other stuff old dykes laughed about, like going deaf or thinking the light was dim when it was their eyes giving out, or forgetting something, or having heartburn after they ate spaghetti? They had some sense of humor. People like them made up the saying "Funny as a crutch" I bet.

Marnie kept whispering, like a prayer, "Ginseng! Ginseng!" all the while she gave her knees a quick treatment with her palms. It really works. Put your palms, left palm is best, on bare skin over pain and the pain stops. I would have done it for her, but her pantlegs were tapered tight and I'd have had to reach inside the top of her pants and embarrass her, not to mention Patricia wouldn't have let me.

Marnie said, "It's come back! Ginseng was hunted to extinction in the nineteenth century for the Chinese market, and here it is back, a whole bunch of it!"

Mother Two said, "The Chinese didn't think much of our little upstart unConfucian ginseng, though, right?"

"Oh no! Wrong! It's the best," Marnie said. "It's the best in the world. Wild Catskill ginseng is the *pinnacle* of Chinese medicine. Listen, Sharon. This is a *treasure*. It is a divine gift, and besides it brings five hundred and sixty dollars a pound wholesale, and if you protect it and don't overharvest it, well, there you are."

If Grandma had known that, she wouldn't have had to make those damn coffee-can pincushions and cut her hands.

Mother Two said, "You have to gather it by moonlight, right?"

"You do not have to gather it by moonlight. But you mustn't be a pig and take too much. The trouble is, the power is in the root. It's not like you can just snip off some leaves. You have to *uproot* it. And it takes seven years to get big enough. You have to know what you're doing. You have to be *reverent* toward it. You have to talk to it and listen when it answers and give it whatever it says it needs."

I was beginning to feel a little bad about giving up the farm, even though I didn't think I'd ever be able to hear what a plant said to me. I felt a little jealous at the idea of *my* ginseng talking to somebody else, even Marnie. They'd be yakking it up beside the waterfalls, and I'd be standing on the subway platform under the city.

But it wouldn't have been fair to back out, after all the trouble Marnie had been to, and anyway she was the one who made me want to keep the place, so I said, trying to sound happy, "Looks like you're going to buy a farm."

"I'm thinking. I'm very close to saying yes. But it's so far from town. But if you're determined to sell it, I can't let some Apeneck Sweeney get hold of it. Oh, Sharon, keep it! I'll buy whatever you'll sell me. Ginseng root, goldenseal root, which is almost as precious. Make me some comfrey ointment. Make me some tincture of motherwort. Don't let go of this place. Please."

I knew better than to get carried away just because Marnie got carried away, but I couldn't stop myself and I didn't want to. I was as excited as Marnie. I wanted to dance and yell, "Yes! Yes! I'll do it!" but instead I said, like some old careful guy that never goes out without his galoshes, "We can't live here. Patricia has to have Washington Square to sell her paintings in."

Patricia said, "If I'll do oil on canvas, I can live anywhere. I've got a gallery."

I said, "You can't. You told me it would wither your hand, like school did."

"I think I've been a little divine flame-y about all that."

It's hard for Patricia to change her mind so I held my breath, afraid Mother Two would ruin everything by saying, "Told you so!" or something.

But she kept still for once, and Patricia said, "I've been experimenting with thinned-down oils. They're not very different from watercolors. And they look nice and blurry and deep and jewelly as the layers build up. The only problem is, they take longer to dry."

"That's not much of a problem," Marnie said.

"That's what I mean — no problem."

I said, "Patricia, remember? When I asked you what's that great smell? And you said, 'Turpentine'? And just let it drop? Why didn't you tell me you'd switched to oils so we could live in the country?"

Her expression reminded me of how she looked as a kid when she conned her father, sort of a simple innocent satisfied look.

She said, "Didn't I promise I'd say no more? To you?" And she looked at Marnie and Mother Two and they all choked back some snickers and gave up and busted out laughing.

They had conned me. Patricia had organized them to con me. I'd been open and sincere with them, but

they hadn't been the same back at me. They'd been
smiling behind my back, watching me get hooked on
my own farm. I had to ask, did they think Mother
One really liked antique cow manure? Oh, yes. Was
wild Catskill ginseng really the pinnacle of Chinese
medicine? *Yes!* Would Marnie really buy our herbs?
Yes yes yes.

I'd rather not have been conned, but it's very
hard to stay mad at a plot to make you happy,
especially when you can always say no if you still
want to.

Marnie was about to trade in her car anyway, so
instead she swapped it with us for half a pound of
ginseng root, which she would dig for herself in the
fall, and five of Patricia's watercolors. The car was
the smallest imaginable yellow Honda, hardly bigger
than a washing machine, but Marnie claimed it had
carried the entire New York University women's
basketball team including substitutes and coach, to
out-of-town games, which they won, and it could
carry anything we asked it to.

Sure enough, when we unbolted the legs, the table
Patricia had brought back from the dead slipped into
the hatchback pretty good. Our clothes in plastic
garbage bags and Patricia's art things and the afghan
filled in the chinks. We left the bed and dishes and
stuff on the street for somebody else to get the good
of. We'd have Grandma's to use.

Then we climbed the stairs one last time to thank

our little home for the happy times it gave us and kiss it goodbye, that is, to kiss each other in every corner and say goodbye, thank you.

The whole neighborhood had our new address and Patricia's warm invitations to come see us. We left, me driving, to a lot of loving waves and good lucks, right after the morning rush-hour traffic. When we crossed the George Washington Bridge, I tooted dear New York goodbye on the horn, which went cheep-cheep like a new-hatched bird, so I wanted to name the car Chick, but Patricia said naming cars is whimsical and wouldn't let me.

The house was about like Grandma left it, just dusty, even though it hadn't been locked. In fact, it had no key. Nobody'd swiped anything or broken anything, but they did leave quite a few used condoms around. I used sticks like tongs to pick them up and put them into a paper bag, feeling so sorry for straights for all they went through, that I didn't even mind very much. I just thought, "Better you than me," until some that hadn't been tied began to spill. Yuck! Old semen stinks like rotten fish, proving once again, Patricia said, that people are oceans. With her that cool, I could stop yelling *"Yuck!"* without being afraid she'd think I had no standards.

While Patricia put her table together, I drove to Mote to phone the power company and get the electricity turned on. Without it to run the pump, we didn't even have water. Sometimes it seems truly crazy to let everything depend that way on a few breakable little wires. Some people can't even use their furnaces without electricity to run the blowers. Some people can't even keep warm in *bed* without electricity to run their blankets. You'd think nobody but Patricia and me ever crouched under a school desk practicing for The Bomb.

When I got back, Patricia had picked out a room to be her studio, and already swept and dusted it and made it pretty with her tubes of paint laid out like organ keys in a curve on her table. I didn't have the heart to tell her she'd freeze in there, come winter. There were several months yet before she needed to know that. The main thing then was *space* — that she wouldn't have to put her paints away so we could eat at the table, that our new home had lots of room. We could have one room for just inhaling and another for just exhaling, if we wanted to.

She had also plugged her little plastic radio into a light cord hanging from the middle of the ceiling. While I was wondering if we'd ever find enough ginseng to pay for more wiring, the radio began to crackle. The electricity was on.

I went outside to thank the man on the power pole for being so quick. He was Kenny, the handsomest, most popular boy in my high school class. He had a big black beard now, like a bad guy's mask, so I didn't recognize him. But he knew me and yelled down for all my news.

What was he doing here? Didn't kids who grew up in Mote get out as fast as they could, like Pa? I'd forgotten to worry about classmates, maybe friendly

unlike back in school, maybe lonesome, maybe horny.
All I'd thought about was living among plants, not
the animal kingdom, except for Patricia and the
women living in twos across the countryside.

Luckily Mote's idea of all your news is no more
than would be in your obituary — are you married
and how many kids do you have? Kenny had one,
who was all boy. You can also talk about your cold
and say the weather is nice/funny. Bad news is, you
went to college.

I said, "I've been living in New York. I just
finished up at City College."

"Figures," he said, very bored. I was notorious in
Mote for studying.

"We're going to raise herbs," I said.

"Uh huh."

He kept his pole-climbing spikes on, sort of like a
doctor keeping his stethoscope around his neck, and
clanked to the house to read the meter. Patricia had
the radio turned up very loud, fiddles and flutes from
WAMC, Albany. She had found it right away.

Getting into his truck, Kenny asked, "You like
that kind of stuff?"

I said, "Oh, *yes!*" I really was getting so I did, a
little. Handel and Mozart anyway.

"And they say *rock 'n' roll* is all the same!" he
said, and looked happy when he wheeled away,
probably because he had me stumped, because I didn't
have an answer to that one, college or not. (I figured
whatever Pa would think, Kenny would think.)

Patricia said, "Well, you got rid of him without
making an enemy of him. Good for you."

I said, "Yes, but it sort of went against the grain.

I'd rather have everybody think I'm interesting, even men."

She said, "Men are trained to believe they have a natural right to whatever they want. So it's best not to show how interesting you are, when you live miles and miles from anywhere."

In a movie, the background music would have turned spooky.

The sun was setting, turning the light that gorgeous yellow that makes all the reds redder and the greens greener, like technicolor or sunglasses, very beautiful except it meant next came night, on the edge of the earth, miles and miles from anywhere, when you're used to a city that never stops vibrating, whose mighty heart never lies still.

We felt too much air around us.

We left the kitchen light on all night, to tell the condom people to stay out.

We didn't make love.

We didn't sleep naked, but wore sweatpants and sweatshirts to bed.

I never knew how citified we had become until we didn't feel as safe around frogs as around junkies.

Next morning, suddenly, without expecting to, we turned sane. Patricia said it was because nobody, at least nobody with a dear lover, could be crazy on a lovely sunny spring morning. When I said it might be because Grandma had come to be our Helper, Patricia looked so impatient that I didn't argue. I just shut up and believed my feeling.

Patricia doesn't always have to be butch or femme or mama or expert, but she does have to be the only nutty theorist. She looks at anybody else's nutty theories very rationally, like Socrates, cornering you point by point, until I understand why the Athenians killed him. I would have too.

We were never scared again, in any weather, night or any time, so doesn't that kind of point to Grandma?

CHAPTER TWO:
Patricia

Sharon thought I was incapable of admiring anybody, because everybody seemed trivial and ricky-ticky next to God and all history — presidents and senators and heroes and poets and queens, even princesses.

So Sharon really blinked when I said, "I admire Marnie." We were digging blue cohosh roots in the woods beside the creek, between the hayfield and the woods.

"Have you gone soft?" Sharon asked.

Daddy used to say, " 'If a man knows how to make a cup of coffee, to such a man I can talk.' " It was a quote from some sage. Even with low standards like that, you don't get too many chances to admire. I admired Marnie because she knew about medicinal herbs, without once imagining she knew *all* about them.

She and a few people like her had somehow intuited that plants and animals are the two halves of a perfect creation, that everything we need for a perfect animal life is in plants. It was as though the mystic hour came round and the Great Goddess summoned her people with a communal dream.

They went to the Library of Congress and studied the quaint volumes of forgotten lore, some true, most not, without knowing which was which, without knowing what plants the old names referred to, loading their minds with things they knew they'd have to forget. What the old witches knew was not in books. They took it to the stake with them.

Marnie was a disappointed opera singer clinging to the outer edges of music by giving piano lessons. She went to Chinatown when her summons came, she went to Indian reservations, knowing nobody there would feel wrong about lying to a paleface. She went to the Ozarks, and to the last surviving ancient Shaker women at Sabbathday Lake in Maine, gathering up what was left of the scattered knowledge. She began to try out the safest-seeming plants, the everyday ones that grew everywhere, dandelion, plantain, chicory, Queen Anne's lace, shepherd's purse, ground ivy, first on herself, then on her lovers and her mother, and kept records. She moved to the country with a group of women and they wildcrafted some herbs and planted others. She moved back to the city alone and created a market, by teaching, by writing, by showing her honest face and her beautiful animal energy in her shop.

By the time Sharon and I came along, the hard part was over.

I said, "I admire Marnie because thanks to her, we know what to do with this blue cohosh."

Marnie had forbidden us to attempt ginseng, golden seal, wild lady slipper, or bethroot until she was on the premises to supervise, personally, every move we made. The blue cohosh was less rare and precious, all right for beginners.

She put her instructions on a cassette tape, which we played over and over on a machine she was throwing out because the automatic stop didn't work anymore. Otherwise it was perfect. Sharon didn't quite want a broken thing. I took it anyway. I became the automatic stop.

To us, that tape was a holy book of the right kind, nothing improbable you had to believe to avoid damnation, just practical and specific, from the Goddess to us by way of a sensible priestess. We stuck to Marnie's instructions like ducklings following their duck and had the problems religions always have, differences of interpretation.

I said, "We aren't supposed to clean the roots with water. They've got too much water in them already. They'll mold. Just brush them with a dry vegetable brush."

Sharon said, "A little water when the dirt's too stuck's okay. It's necessary."

I said, "We shouldn't cut up the roots."

Sharon said, "If they're thick we should."

Was blue cohosh thick? How thick was thick?

The tape said Marnie chopped, with her big salad-chopping knife, burdock root because it was an inch and a half thick. Did that mean anything thinner than that wasn't thick enough to chop? We disagreed.

We agreed on buying a few yards of nylon screening, the window kind, which we made clumsy bundles of cohosh in, disagreeing on how many roots per bundle, and then on where to hang them.

"Above the woodstove," Sharon said.

"That's when you have a high ceiling," I said. "You want to bake them?"

We could disagree all day without anybody's being declared a heretic or tortured. What other religion can you say that for? And after the supper dishes were washed, we'd go to bed and listen to the tape again, both saying, "See? See?" happy and justified and smiling and kissing, warm in our creaky bed. Spring nights in Greene County can be cold, but we weren't.

One night while I was nuzzling Sharon's breast, confidently, with no sense of privilege, like a well-loved baby, "The Messiah" came flying down from Albany on a flawless FM signal, though Easter was past and Christmas far off, an unaccountable gift. Eileen Farrell sang "I Know That My Redeemer Liveth," and I felt Sharon listening with every cell of her body, feeling every breath and rise and fall. Then Eileen ended.

"I love women's voices," Sharon said, and breathed the orchestra part across my ear, not into it, across it, as across a flute, and my body became the music and rose and dipped and soared, never in danger of being lost because safely anchored at her breast.

One night I wanted to try something I'd read about in a book called *Love Secrets of Araby,* though it went against my principles to bring an alien object into lovemaking. If your body and her body aren't enough for you, you shouldn't be making love, I always thought, but it's humbling and educational to go against your principles now and then. You're less smug. You're more tolerant. And in this case the object was a mere orange, a big bright innocent California navel orange, which I tossed from hand to hand, humming casually to get Sharon's attention, and then sexily peeled with bites and tugs. Inside that thick peel, it was small, like an Eskimo with her furs off. I broke it along its seams. With my fingertips I pressed Sharon, who was very interested and curious and yielding, backward to the bed, saying in my all-purpose foreign accent, "Eef you do as I say, you vill come to no harm." If you're going to ask a woman to have no one but you, you should make sure she doesn't have to do without something she might want, such as a French lover.

I nudged her thighs apart with my face, but when I tried to put the orange section inside her she clamped them shut again. She had a very naive impression of anatomy, like the first women to use tampons, who were afraid the tampons would get into their bloodstreams and hit their hearts and kill them.

I had to stop right there, at such an exciting part, and remind her how snug and contained it is in there, how there was no place for the orange to go except right back out again.

"Bot uff course, vee need not do eet eef you do not vish to."

"No, I'm up for it," she said, and doubtingly squeaked herself open enough to let me slip in the piece of orange.

Then at last the fiery sultan could begin the intoxicating part, the whole idea, sucking it out. I sucked. I sucked. I tried to reach it with my tongue. I sucked some more.

"You shit!" she cried. "You can't get it out!"

"Uff course I can. Eet is not supposed to be immediate. Thees is vat is callt 'foreplay.' I could easily remoof it weeth my feenger, bot then I vould haff to turn in my sultan shirt."

So she began to laugh a big hearty laugh, saying, "I'll have to go plant marigolds tomorrow with a goddamn *orange* in me," and the laugh pressed her innards down and out popped the orange. I ate it and made love to her the old usual way, with my hand. We didn't need the variations of Araby. We were far from saying, "Oh, no! Ambrosia *again?*"

Marnie couldn't stay away. She rolled in every Saturday evening, bringing us things she'd lain awake worrying about our not having, such as a three-beam scale, and a box of empty cotton drawstring teabags for us to fill, and a gross of one-ounce eye-dropper-type amber glass bottles, and a gallon of laboratory alcohol, which we couldn't buy but she could because she had a New York State re-sale number.

It was a relief to stop trying to dry those blue cohosh roots and simply chop them up and tincture them, which means soaking them in alcohol a few weeks, eight ounces per quart. The plant's energy goes into the alcohol, ready to be dripped, ten drops per cup, into boiling water, and when it cools down a little, drunk. The alcohol goes up in steam. We had a cellarful of Danica's blue canning jars just right for tincturing.

Marnie was a good guest, not fussy, and if she brought a lover it was always one who was also not fussy. She brought food, too. But she began to scare us, spending our money before we had any.

"I'll take it out in trade," she said, and of course that was the only possibility, but it meant we'd be erasing debt instead of getting money for a while.

Sharon and I both have a real dislike of debt, she because her parents were always behind and worried, I because my parents never were. Debt goes against the Burley Family's sturdy-yeoman Jeffersonian image, and I have never stopped being a Burley even when Sharon laughs at me and says, "So what? Everybody's *some*thing."

So even though we needed everything Marnie brought us, and there was not one luxury in the lot, and she certainly was not dunning us, she did scare me into taking afternoons to paint, and Sharon got a job she saw an ad for on the bulletin board in the store.

* * * * *

I was curious about what country life would do to
my pictures. Would I do barns and hills? But except
for maybe an increase of flowers, the pictures stayed
much the same, fish and angels and birds, new again
because I had to teach the oil paints to do what I
wanted.

On top of one of the front porch pillars was a
robins' nest passionately watched over by both
parents. They'd sit on the power line and watch us,
scowling nervously, and decide we were too close and
suddenly rush us, buzz us, especially after the babies
hatched. I got one pretty good thump on the head.
After that I put a box over my head if I couldn't
avoid going out front. I was afraid they'd get my
eyes. They were hawks at heart, brave and noble no
doubt, but in the end tiresome.

"Listen!" I yelled from safe inside the screen door,
"we're not going to hurt your babies, and you should
know that. How has your race survived through the
ages if you can't tell a friend from an enemy? If you
didn't trust us, you shouldn't have built your nest so
damn close!"

Sharon took my outburst harder than the robins
did. I was afraid she might cry.

"Don't be mad at the robins," she pleaded, and of
course I forgave them instantly for her sake, or
thought I did, but birds got rarer in my pictures.

You never think to be scared of robins. You never
hear how butchy they are. Bees didn't sting us if we
moved slowly, and snakes slid away if we let them
know we were coming. The only ones on the whole

farm that went out of their way for a fight were those two killer robins.

A lot of herbs were suddenly ready at once. We tinctured the fresh young leaves of motherwort. Comfrey we strung up to dry on hooks in the barn, like tobacco. In a week the leaves were ready to be stripped off the stems and crumbled and stored in fruit jars. The same with the Saint John's wort and the boneset and mullein. It was getting nerve-wracking, everything coming so fast like that, leaves getting too coarse, going to waste.

Marnie said, "Take it *easy*. If a plant lies on the ground and becomes its elements again, it is not wasted. You share the common human delusion that anything that doesn't pass through the human bowel is wasted."

Yes, we did think that, but we began right then to try not to. Sometimes it was hard not to worry and hurry, but we achieved what we called a steady hiker's pace. It was that or go crazy.

Then we could enjoy moving gently among the bees and clipping our herb stems with pruning shears and carrying our harvest in willow laundry baskets to the big harvest table in the barn. Meditative. We became meditative.

Marnie liked to play the old Mason and Hamlin organ, mostly Bach because that was what she knew by heart, "Sheep May Safely Graze" and "Jesu, Joy of Man's Desiring," which we never got tired of but she did, a little. She wanted to branch out, so she

opened one of Danica's brittle yellow hymnbooks and
out fell a five-dollar bill.

That got us interested as well as pleased, and we
made a detailed search. From between the plates in
the dish cupboard, from the folds of clean sheets,
from books, from rolled-up pairs of socks, from under
linoleum, from a sack of sugar, old Danica's
squirrelings came fluttering.

Was there ever a woman who trusted this man's
world, who didn't have a stash somewhere, in the
certain knowledge that no ship ever returned, no
child lived to adulthood, no farmer made a crop, no
barn escaped burning, no back didn't slip a disc?

Danica's stash was nine hundred and fifteen
dollars, all in small bills. It was lots easier to be
meditative then.

It was time to be social. One mustn't overload
one's relationship and all that. Let there be spaces in
your togetherness and all that. If you wait till you're
caught up, you wait forever. It was time to call Fran
and Dot and ask how the rosebushes were doing and
get us invited to a dyke potluck.

I couldn't find their number. It had to be in my
address book, but wasn't. Somehow in the move I had
mislaid that slip of paper. It had to be in one of the
garbage bags. I finished the unpacking without
finding it. It had to be in the pocket of the shirt I
wore the day I met them, if I could remember which
shirt it was and if it hadn't been through the wash a
dozen times since.

I couldn't remember Fran and Dot's last names.

That information was on the paper with their phone number, somewhere in the Atlantic Ocean.

I looked for them in every passing pickup truck, and lurked extra at the store. It was maddening to know our people were all around us, hidden like water in the ground, and we could die of thirst before we found them.

Well, I could find someone else, the same way I'd found Fran and Dot in the first place.

She was about sixty, a fine tall massive lady with a gray crewcut. She was buying yellow stomping boots at the general store. Aha.

I said, nice weather, herbs, my friend Sharon, Greenwich Village, blah blah blah, while she showed no hurry to get away.

I said, "Oh, by the way — is there any social life around here for us?"

"Oh, *yes!*" she said. "Our young people's group at church is *very* active. The mister and I never miss a get-together."

"Uh, well —" I said. "I'll certainly keep that in mind. Young people's group. Um hum."

She laughed. "It's the whole congregation. Nobody will admit they're not young anymore."

"Well, thanks. Thanks a lot. I'll certainly keep it in mind."

I sidled off, defeated. You just can't tell by looking, in the country.

CHAPTER THREE:
Sharon

I began being an odd-job person when some people wanted their roof gutters cleaned out. Thanks to Grandma, I wasn't scared of heights. In fact, I have a pretty good head for heights, within reason, and even though the people would rather not have hired a woman, they took me because no man answered their ad.

While I was on the roof I noticed some loose flashing, and they said, "Okay, fix it," and I did.

They turned out to need their windowframes caulked, too, and a ceiling patched and the room repainted, and the grass cut and marigolds planted. They were weekend people from Albany, state government people. They didn't know you didn't have to pay ten bucks an hour for those jobs in Mote, but I figured a college graduate was worth it.

They were college graduates too, I suppose, but so dumb. They showed how far people had fallen from real life and how important it was to get back. For instance, when they saw the lettuce I planted for them, just up, two leaves, they said, "But where's the head? Is it underground?" They had a thing about underground. When they saw a wheatfield they said, "But where's the bread? Is it underground?"

I explained as nicely as I could, not letting on they were idiots. They looked like I was lying and said, "How do *you* know?" So I felt okay about the ten bucks an hour.

I could do simple plumbing, like putting in new faucet washers and opening drains and stopping leaks, and simple carpentry, like replacing rotten steps, so I thought, why not? and put my own ad on the bulletin board in the store.

That's when we got a phone. "Call evenings," I had to say, because it rang so much it drove Patricia nuts while she was painting. Of course the country people didn't need me, but lots of poor dumb weekenders from Albany did. I think they hardly knew how to change a lightbulb.

I built a lot of patios for weekenders, dug out the sod and laid bricks. They liked to have their drinks on their patios and look out across what they called The Land, which was grass one inch tall and

marigolds and a clipped hedge and then if they were
the very luckiest, the mountains. It was all right, I
guess, but they thought they were roughing it, really
in the heart of nature. The main thing they worried
about was somebody putting a house-trailer where
they might see it. They kept wanting to buy more
land so nobody ever could.

One lot of them was just down the road from us.
In fact, they'd bought their Land from Grandma, five
acres that they civilized hell out of. They began to
hint about our place.

"Of course we understood that your grandmother
wasn't physically *able* —" they'd say. Maybe it was
stronger than hinting? "You're very welcome to
borrow the mower," they'd say — as if I'd let that
monster with its stinking fumes anywhere near our
herbs! "You know there are lots of noxious pests and
weed seeds that winter over in rubble," they'd say,
meaning that all the weeds and bugs in the
neighborhood came from Patricia and me not mowing.

It did bother me to have somebody — all right,
*any*body — think we were slummy and trashy, but I
also knew they were wrong, and that one-inch grass
was stupid, and anyway the robins wouldn't let us
into our front yard.

We sure weren't lazy. Every week we had
tinctures or teabags or chopped-up dandelion roots or
something ready for Marnie to take back to the Rose
Hip. As soon as Patricia's oil paintings got dry she
started sending them to town with Marnie, too. They
were so beautiful, maybe more even than the old
watercolors, deeper and glowier, that I could hardly

stand to see them go, but Patricia claimed to be a tough pro.

"I'd sell my grandmother," she said, which still didn't explain how she could sell her paintings, but I shut up, not to make it harder for her.

The gallery the Mothers had found for her on West Fourth Street, Marnie said, always had something by Patricia in its window, where beauty and low price and lots of tourists passing by made sales quick. Pretty soon Marnie was bringing money to Patricia, first a piddle, then a flow. Even though the gallery kept most of the money, what was left was more than Patricia had ever dared ask for in Washington Square.

And of course I was doing pretty good odd-jobbing it, enough so I could get a little uppity and turn people down if I didn't like them, for instance the ones that wanted us to mow our grass.

We were also going on with Grandma's beast business, casting in her old molds, but the demand was kind of slow, maybe because when the grass got really tall the beasts didn't show up.

There was winter to think of, too, mainly the wood the old woodstove would want. There was plenty of Grandma's left in the woodshed, seasoned and ready, a year old. Next year's winter was what we had to bring in wood for. We could get it in the woodlot, no problem, but Patricia said we had to not be grasshoppers and wait till the snow flew to do it.

I thought a heat wave was a funny time to worry about snow two winters away, but Patricia said no.

"It is the exactly right time," she said. "The

lesson of a heatwave is that nature is never moderate. With nature, it's too much or nothing. Floods or droughts."

When Patricia's in the mood to find the lesson of something, you just have to curl up and wait for it to go away. She should have been a teacher. She sounded just like one who was about to flunk me.

"The human problem is how to use the times of excess to prepare for the opposites that are sure to come."

Um hum.

We tied bandannas around our heads to keep the sweat out of our eyes and headed for the woods with our rented chain saw, which threw off a lot of blue fumes too, like a lawnmower, but the saw was necessary and a mower wasn't. At the edge of the woods, as far as possible from the ginseng and golden seal, we picked out a young maple with a trunk about six inches thick and had it down in no time.

"There's hundreds more," we said. "They need thinning," we said, but still felt like we'd shot a doe, like we'd sold our grandmother.

You do get tough, though. Before we had that tree de-boughed and dragged to the yard, it felt like an enemy. Then we had to go back for another one. And another. And another. And change our sweatbands. And drink a gallon of water. And go back for another tree.

"Grandma always paid a man to do this," I said, stupidly. Patricia had been almost ready to give up until I said that.

* * * * *

Patricia looked and looked for our people, but it
was me that found them. I mean, I found the first
ones and they led to all the rest.

Even on the phone asking me to build her some
bookshelves, Stacy sounded like a dyke. "She has a
lesbian accent," I told Patricia, who was still so
embarrassed about misjudging that old church lady
that she just grumbled.

"I bet," she grumbled. "In the country you can't
tell. Anyway, a dyke could build her own bookshelves."

"Yeah, but these are weekenders, from *Albany,*" I
said.

Stacy and Edra were about the age of the Mothers
and Marnie, I think. Actually, after a certain point
they all look alike. Stacy and Edra had two bedrooms,
one just basic and dusty and the other human-
smelling and full of angel statues and two sizes of
clothes on bamboo hooks and two sizes of shoes
beside a chair and books I thought it wouldn't be
polite to be too curious about the titles of. Looking
across the huge bed was Venus de Milo with fresh-cut
roses at her feet. She was really beautiful. I'd never
realized. There was some of Patricia in how she was
ancient and young at the same time.

That bedroom was where they needed more
shelves. I measured and figured surrounded by
pictures of women. I don't mean naked. I mean faces,
a whole wall of faces, which Stacy said were Rosa
Bonheur and Queen Anne and Gertrude Stein and
Alice B. Toklas and Romaine Brooks and Natalie
Barney and Ethel Smyth and Sara Teasdale and Alice
Austin and Djuna Barnes and Berenice Abbott and I

can't remember who all. One named Colette glared at me like she knew I was no damn good. I'd never heard of any of them except Susan B. Anthony. Her at least I recognized.

I made Stacy and Edra sad. "Every generation starts over," they said.

Later I saw they could just have been talking about women's rights, and I could have put my foot in it like Patricia did with the church lady, who was still hoo-hooing at us every time we passed and saying she was expecting us next Sunday.

But at the time I was sure Stacy and Edra meant, damn it, why don't young lesbians know their own history? (Susan B. *Anthony?* Now I'd *really* have to vote!)

I cut and sanded and stained and waxed my shelf boards under a pear tree out back, thinking what Patricia would say if she'd been there. She would noodle and wait and hint around and back off and ooze back, and I thought that was a good idea. That was the way I'd do it too.

I went back inside to put up the shelf brackets, a very simple job except for finding the studs but I was good at that. My ears could really tell the difference between one tap on the wall and another.

Edra was playing the piano but she stopped to ask if I needed anything, an extension cord maybe.

I said, "Do you know some women named Fran and Dot? Patricia lost their phone number. They told her you have potlucks."

* * * * *

The next potluck was on a Saturday night, so Marnie came with us. There were about thirty women of all ages there, including Fran and Dot who got to know Marnie at last, just like they'd always wanted to back at the Rose Hip. "We used to follow you sometimes, to see if you'd lead us to our people," they said.

I thought that might piss Marnie, but she understood. She said, "I read in a book that gay people hung out at Riis Park, so I went there when I first hit town. But it was in May. The wind off the Atlantic was still awfully cold, and nobody was out yet."

Edra said, "I read in a book that lesbians hung out on Sixth Avenue in the Village and jumped you, so I used to walk there very slowly, and stop and pretend to study the store windows, hoping and hoping —"

Somebody else said, "I used to make one beer last five hours in a Mafia bar. Those bars were rough. The old butches were always getting into fist fights. You had to keep your eyes downturned, not to accidentally look at somebody's femme, or you'd get invited outside and clobbered."

Somebody else said, "The Mafia got kind of sick of the fist fights and one beer in five hours. It hardly paid them to bribe the cops, for what they got out of us. The gay guys were who had the money."

Somebody else said, "One night an old butch pulled up at the bar in a cab and as it was pulling away she ran after it, yelling, 'My dildo! My dildo!' She caught up with the cab and came back with a little canvas bag like you take your stuff to the gym in."

Patricia and I enjoyed it all, laughing when they did, but knowing better than to believe everything, like about the cops having to be bribed. We knew it was the number old-timers always pull, about what they went through that, thanks to their pioneering, *we* don't have to go through. We were supposed to feel like a thinning-out of the old breed, soft and pampered, everything easier than we deserved.

But we were too glad about being there in a real country lesbian home in a room packed solid with lesbians, not one alien in sight, to feel like reminding them that it was Baby Boomers, mostly, who got our women out of the bars and stomped and yelled and confronted and demanded and got arrested and made the rules start changing for us for the first time since the Isle of Lesbos.

I think, all in all, it's probably better to be at one of our potlucks than on the Isle of Lesbos, though it's sweet to think of all those poets reaching inside each other's little gowns in the sunshine with olive trees and blue sea all around. That may seem better than sitting cross-legged on a rug with whoever can still get down there, eating off a bendy paper plate with a plastic fork, though the food is delicious — lasagna and ham and tiny meatballs in dill sauce and ripe tomatoes and something called kufta that is *great,* and dolmas and saffron rice and potato salad and a dozen desserts including chocolate brownies that Sappho would have killed for.

But you could get sick of nothing but poets, I suspect, and be glad to have only one, like we have, and have all the rest be other stuff. We have teachers

and secretaries and social workers and physical
therapists and store clerks and bus drivers and nurses
and lawyers and accountants and government people
weekending from Albany and shrinks, lots of shrinks.
One shrink said her clients, who are children, keep
ripping the penises off her anatomically-correct father
dolls, so when she interviews prospective secretaries
she has to ask, "Can you sew penises back on?" We
have one dentist. We have one college dean. Patricia
gave us one painter. I gave us one odd-jobber.

Marnie said, "No, no, you are an *herbalist,*" like
that was better than odd-jobber, which I guessed it
was natural for her to think. Would the other women
think so too, and not be as proud of me as I was of
them?

After all the garbage you can hear even now —
about being sick, or immature, or better-off dead, or
lesbian life is one long mess — it's pretty nice to
have living proof that it's not so, to know all these
cheerful, funny, good-looking, smart lesbians who take
good care of themselves in the world, *succeed,* and
take good care of each other and their kids in nice
houses snuggled here and there in the woods and
mountains. Not a one lives right in Mote. Naturally
we wanted to look good too, for their sake and our
own. Patricia was no problem. "Painter" always
sounds good, especially when you can mention an
actual gallery in New York City. But "odd-jobber" is
borderline. At best.

I was a very good odd-jobber and proud of it, but
we were both still kind of shaky as herbalists. There
was so much to learn, that I could have learned while
I worked at the Rose Hip if I hadn't been going to
City College to try to stop being an unlicked cub. We

needed long slow snowy winter days beside the
woodstove, to read and make lists — really seriously,
at last, to *study* herbs. To learn their botanical
names, for starters. Their dangers and uses. By heart.
Down cold. Like Marnie. And then check it all out
with real plants and real people. Have an educated
opinion on Hildegarde of Bingen and Nicholas
Culpeper, and Maud Grieve. "Maud Grieve says blah
blah, but in my experience —" Impressive stuff like
that was years away.

But — Marnie said, "No, no, you are an
herbalist." Not "will be" but "are." After always
thinking she knew best, should I start contradicting
her?

I gave us one herbalist.

Patricia, because she didn't know as much as God,
refused to make it two.

What a difference those women make! They are
what makes it possible to live in the country. Is it
their hugs and kisses hello and goodbye? Their easy
laughter? Their wonderful food? Their love-filled
homes? The health they prove is possible? Their
fearless aging? Their plain human beauty? Their
rowdy singing around old upright pianos? Their
intelligence? Yes, but something more. They are the
family that's glad you two got together. They are the
father that's proud you're a girl. To them it is
central, correct, and blessed to be a girl. And
something more yet. They are there. Some months we
don't even go, too tired, too busy. It doesn't matter.

They are *there*. They bring our world up to size and round it out.

The funny part was that when I said I was an herbalist and nobody laughed, I sort of began to be one. I guess the shrinks have known for a long time that people tend to act like they're expected to, but *I* didn't know it until women at the potlucks began asking my advice and I had some to give. I sure never thought I could know more without having to learn more, just because somebody expected me to.

First it was Edra, who you might think would have been stuck at the idea of me as odd-jobber, but no. She said she'd had a rash on the calf of her right leg every winter for years. Her doctor had given her cortisone ointment for it. My God, a hormone for an *itch?* You don't have to be Einstein to know better than to play with hormones, do you? It worked, but the rash came right back afterwards. Some natural good sense kept Edra from going back for more cortisone. She stopped the itching by squirting very hot water on it, so she stayed comfortable.

"But, damn, I'd like to be rid of the rash," she said.

"Comfrey ointment," I said. I swear it came out of nowhere.

It really made my reputation.

Stacy, who'd had four children, got urinary frequency every January. I guess it's miserable. It's feeling you have to pee all the time but just getting a few drops out. Her doctor said, Oh, yes, multiparous

women do tend to get that in winter, ho ho. He gave
her sulfa for it. But wasn't sulfa dangerous? Couldn't
it crystalize in your kidneys and block them?

"Uva ursi," I said, which wasn't as remarkable
because by then it was winter and we had time to
study.

A lot will change.

Patricia's gallery will hire a publicity agent to
make her famous. She will be slightly glad, though
she always meant to be an amateur. We'll like the
money.

Our families will move with the times and come
to believe that homosexuality is perfectly all right for
other people's families. If Patricia grieves about not
being able to go to the Old Place, she will not tell
me.

I will become able to say I'm an herbalist without
thinking I'm lying. We will be healers and teachers,
with dewy sparkly strong young women around us as
apprentices.

And then? And then?

Then there'll be something else, and something
else.

Next time we'll be born on the same day. I'm
eager to do it all again, even the sad parts, but
especially that first winter.

That first winter on the farm together stays in
my mind as a perfect little separate world, like an
island, like a tree house. Like a fuzzy submarine, like
a space ship. Like the scene inside a fancy Easter
egg. Like those paperweights you shake and inside

tiny snowflakes fall on tiny houses and pine trees and children singing carols.

And there we are inside our little separate world, in the kitchen that is logs under the plaster. We are like sheep folded warm in their sheepfold, snug as bears, while outside the wind heaps up the snow. On the woodstove, soup is cooking with slow burps. There's stone-ground wheat bread in the oven. The maple fire snaps. The silky brown cats are silkily asleep in each other's arms. Their names are Odetta and Ruby Dee. Alix Dobkin is singing.

No, Patricia is playing her recorder — with difficulty, because my ear is burrowed between her breasts. I listen through long johns, a flannel shirt, and two sweaters to her breath moving in and out. She is playing a hymn, "Now Thank We All Our God."

We are studying. No, we are rocking salad knives through dried burdock root. No, it's barberry. No, it's purple sunflower.

That yellow blur is our Honda rusting in the barn. Her headlights are held on with silver duct tape. She wants to be red dust, then iron ore, then steel, then a Honda again. Her name is Chick.

No, Patricia is painting. That yellow is the crest of an African crowned crane. That fragrance is turpentine.

The Women's Press is Britain's leading women's publishing house. Established in 1978, we publish high-quality fiction and non-fiction from outstanding women writers worldwide. Our exciting and diverse list includes literary fiction, detective novels, biography and autobiography, health, women's studies, handbooks, literary criticism, psychology and self help, the arts, our popular Livewire Books series for young women and the bestselling annual *Women Artists Diary* featuring beautiful colour and black-and-white illustrations from the best in contemporary women's art.

If you would like more information about our books or about our mail order book club, please send an A5 sae for our latest catalogue and complete list to:

The Sales Department
The Women's Press Ltd
34 Great Sutton Street
London EC1V 0DX
Tel: 0171 251 3007
Fax: 0171 608 1938

Also of interest

Isabel Miller
Patience and Sarah

'A beautifully written lesbian love story.' *Cosmopolitan*

Patience and Sarah met in Connecticut in 1816. Within days they
were lovers...

Based on the lives of American painter Mary Ann Willson and
her companion Miss Brundidge, who farmed, lived and loved
together in the early nineteenth century, *Patience and Sarah* is a
literary and lesbian classic. First published by Isabel Miller herself
in 1969 when she was unable to find a publisher daring enough
to take it on, this much-loved book is now an enduring
international bestseller.

'Funny and true and tender, emotionally and physically
erotic.' *Literary Review*

'This book is a real find.' *Good Housekeeping*

Fiction £5.99
ISBN 0 7043 3848 3

Isabel Miller
The Love of Good Women

From the celebrated author of *Patience and Sarah* comes the
enchanting story of what happened when Gertrude met Milly.

A dutiful wife and mother, Gertrude is convinced she should be
grateful to Earl for marrying her and to her children for loving
her. But to her confusion, Gertrude finds herself drawn to Milly,
her free-spirited sister-in-law and a self-acknowledged lesbian.

It is the last years of World War Two, and apprehensively
Gertrude takes on a wartime factory job. Her new-found
independence brings the companionship of co-workers, the
beginnings of a real friendship with Milly, and her delighted entry
into a world of women and romance she never dreamed
existed...

**'Spare economical prose full of vivid details...Isabel
Miller writes wonderfully.'** *Company*

Fiction £5.99
ISBN 0 7043 4447 5

Isabel Miller
A Dooryard Full of Flowers

From the writer of one of the most cherished books of all time
comes the enchanting continuation of her classic story, *Patience
and Sarah*. Now, in *A Dooryard Full of Flowers*, Isabel Miller offers
long-awaited glimpses of their 'slow, ardent, exalted life
together'.

And meet here too the married woman who falls in love with
her mother-in-law, a woman in the navy determined that this
time she will *not* fall for her new bunkmate, and a woman who
finally comes face-to-face with her long-term penpal with
unexpected results...

**'There is a sense of authenticity which transcends
fiction. Much the same can be said for her characters,
who move through life with an almost stately grace.
Most are seekers, women looking for love in all its
guises... Their issues are the internal struggles of
women, transcending time and era.'** *Lambda Book Report*

Fiction £6.99
ISBN 0 7043 4411 4

Caeia March
Reflections

From the much-loved author of *Three-Ply Yarn*, *The Hide and Seek Files*, *Fire! Fire!* and *Between the Worlds* comes a superb exploration of the power of legend, women's spirituality and erotic love.

Returning home after many months, Vonn Smedley dreams of the legendary romance of Tristan and Iseult. Forced by her father, the King, to make a marriage of political expedience, Iseult falls irrevocably in love with her husband-to-be's envoy. But dreams are no respecter of gender, and Tristan appears to Vonn as Tristanne – a beautiful warrior woman.

Then Vonn meets Rachel and, as the two women are drawn instantly together, myth and reality collide and coalesce...

'March is doing what novels ought to do, using the particularity of fiction to examine, expose, unfurl.'
Sara Maitland, *New Statesman*

'Hers is a unique voice, simultaneously poetic and colloquial.' Joanna Briscoe

'Tantalising, sensual, slow-moving, tender and romantic.'
Gay Community News

'Highly erotic.' *The Cornishman*

Fiction £6.99
ISBN 0 7043 4419 X

Stevie Davies
Closing the Book

For five contented years, Bridie has been Ruth's ally, a steadfast
companion in an increasingly harsh world. Now, without
warning, all has changed, and both the future and history of their
lives together are suddenly, shockingly, called into question...

Closing the Book is Stevie Davies' moving yet ultimately hopeful
exploration of the bitter cruelties of nature and the violence of
man-made suffering. Following the success of her last three
acclaimed novels, this award-winning author offers a beautiful and
powerful story of strength, survival and reconciliation.

**'Relationships are explored with all the subtlety at the
command of this highly original writer who has an
extraordinary insight into the workings of the human
mind and emotions.'** *The Times*

'One of the most uplifting novels I have read for years.'
Everywoman

'Enthralling.' *Guardian*

Fiction £6.99/£12.99
ISBN 0 7043 4388 6 pbk
      0 7043 5064 5 hbk

Jess Wells
AfterShocks

Tracy 'Trout' Giovanni's life is neat, controlled, ferociously
organised. A powerful businesswoman and meticulous
houseowner, she has life's every unpredictable possibility
covered. Then the earthquake – 8.0 on the Richter scale – hits
San Francisco. And Trout's whole world rocks.

Now Trout comes face to face with the chaos she has always,
compulsively, tried to avoid, but which has always been waiting
beneath the cold, hard layer of her self-imposed order. And as
her lover, Patricia, waits in a bar across town for Trout to find
her and to reimpose that safe security she never knew that she
needed, Trout is slowly, inexorably changing...

This beautiful novel takes a tender and evocative look at women
forced to confront their fundamental needs, fears and desires; to
come to terms with their past and its distortions of the present;
and to learn to meet, love and live with each other on the firm,
solid ground of reality.

'This book kept me up all night.' Kate Millett

**'Utterly compelling...Brilliantly written, AfterShocks
subtly evokes the capacity for human endurance and
solidarity. A fine book...strongly recommended.'**
The Pink Paper

Fiction £6.99
ISBN 0 7043 4383 5

Andrea Freud Loewenstein
The Worry Girl
Stories from a Childhood

'When I was young there were pieces I tried to sort out
but could not. My parents' accent, for example, which I
couldn't hear but had to believe because it was the first
thing anyone ever said when they met them... Then
there was being related to Sigmund Freud. He was the
glowering man with a beard in the picture in the living
room. He was a genius and being related to him was
supposed to be a good thing...'

Set in an often-hostile upper-middle-class gentile suburban town,
The Worry Girl is the evocative part-autobiography, part coming-
out novel of one sensitive, assimilated Jewish girl. Movingly, she
tells of her confrontation with the rigid systems of class and
caste at school, and of the no-less-damaging struggle with a well-
meaning but over-loving mother. The Worry Girl is a powerful,
unputdownable autobiographical novel about a girl's triumphant
fight against daily prejudice...a fight that is finally rewarded by her
own movement towards sexual and creative freedom.

'**Compelling, moving and beautifully written.**'
Gay Community News

Fiction/Autobiography £5.99
ISBN 0 7043 4371 1

May Sarton
Mrs Stevens Hears the Mermaids Singing

May Sarton is internationally acclaimed for her novels, *The Magnificent Spinster*, *The Education of Harriet Hatfield*, *A Reckoning*, *A Shower of Summer Days*, *As We Are Now*, *The Single Hound* and *Kinds of Love*, as well as for her bestselling journals, but this classic and much-loved novel has a special significance both to the author herself and to her readers. It is the first in which May Sarton wrote openly about homosexual love.

Hilary Stevens, a formidable personality and renowned poet, is in her seventies. But her hard-worn peace is disrupted first by an angry young poet, Mar, and then by two journalists seeking the source of her inspiration. In the course of her interview with them, and as her relationship with Mar develops, Hilary Stevens finally comes to terms with her own past and her creative muse.

'May Sarton ranks with the very best of distinguished novelists. The reader is compelled to that feeling of awe which the accomplishments of first-rate literary creation inevitably bring forth.' *New York Times Book Review*

Fiction £5.99
ISBN 0 7043 4333 9